LAKE OF BAYS

On Roothog Island

The Chadwick Bay Series

By Jerry Price & Tom Roy

BE REAL MEN
www.2brealmen.com

LAKE OF BAYS

ISBN: 0-9765412-8-9

Unless otherwise indicated, all Scripture quotations are from *Holy Bible*, New Living Translation. © 1996. Used by permission of Tyndale House Publishers, Inc., Wheaton, Illinois 60189.
All rights reserved.

Additional Scripture quotations are from the *King James Version*
Printed in the United States of America ALL RIGHTS
RESERVED

© 2018 by Jerry Price and Tom Roy
2BRealMen Publishing
Jerry@2BRealMen.com & Tom@2BRealMen.com

JERRY PRICE & TOM ROY

Lake Of Bays

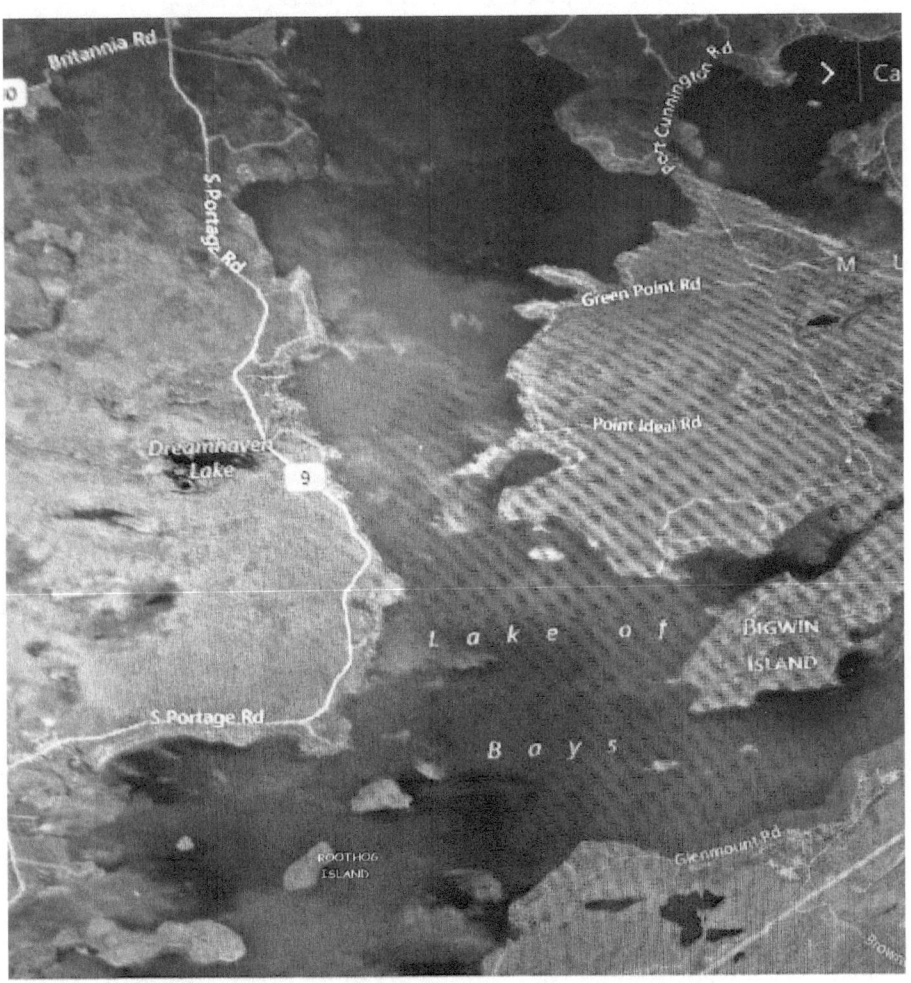

JERRY PRICE & TOM ROY

What Others Are Saying

Jerry and Tom remind men of the importance of honest, open relationships in sustaining meaning in life. The formal programming aspects of the main character, Bob's journey, were offset by authentic life circumstances that demanded change. By the end of the story, two things are realized; God is always at work in a man's life and we all need a Roothog Island experience.

JOE URCAVICH
Former chaplain for the Green Bay Packers Public
Speaker, Leadership Coach, Alignment Advisor
www.josephurcavich.com

It was with eager anticipation I dove into reading Lake Of Bays On Roothog Island by Jerry Price and Tom Roy. I couldn't wait to find out where Bob Chadwick would go next. The ride I was taken on was full of twists and turns the likes of which I never expected. This book is more than a story about a fictional character. It is a great tool to help twisted individuals start on the road to becoming real men.

TED BARRETT
MLB crew chief #65

Lake of Bays on Roothog Island brings to a close the latest chapter in Bob Chadwick's life. Once again, Jerry Price and Tom Roy have tapped into the genuine issues that men struggle with; accurately describing the twisted logic we so often fall into.

They do so in a way that does not make men less masculine, but rather resonates with emotions and motivations we feel, but cannot always put into words. The promise of hope with the restoration and redemption we can have as men permeates the story. Even though Lake Of Bays is a short read, it took longer than expected, as I found myself rereading certain passages repeatedly as Bob's struggles and logic so clearly reflected my own. Even in writing this endorsement, Bob's discussion with Simon about the difference between perfection and excellence pops into my mind and I find myself thinking instead of writing. Whether you have read the first two books of the Chadwick Bay Series, or this is your first look into the life of Bob Chadwick, you will soon find something of your own journey in the pages.

DEAN JADERSTON
Executive Director, Northern Pines of Minnesota Men's
Basketball Coach at Sterling College
Sterling, Kansas

Jerry Price and Tom Roy's book, Lake Of Bays On Roothog Island, is an engaging story of a man's breakthrough to spiritual transformation and emotional healing, through the help and love of a group of committed men. Written in an easy-to-read style that most men *and women* can relate to, the book is more than a story. It is an instructive study that invites the reader to consider his or her own need for personal wholeness.

BOB PARKS
Chaplain, Heritage Seminary, Cambridge, ON

FOREWARD

One of the most common complaints men make these days about churches is that the public services, sermons and ministries feel too feminine, even too soft and "nice." They say they feel uncomfortable in an environment that doesn't seem to place a high value or priority on masculinity.

Men instinctively prefer a spiritual community that refuses to soft pedal the message of Jesus. Dumbing down the Bible or making following Jesus easy is the fastest way to turn motivated men off. Real men like to hear truth undiluted and straight from the shoulder.

This book by Price and Roy takes off the kid gloves of watered down easy faith. They have found by their own experience and the reports of other men that raising the bar in positive personal change is actually attractive to men. Those who have found their faith experience a bit feminized in the past will be intrigued by a "tell it the way it is" style of communication.

These authors believe an honest and challenging brand of genuine relationship with our Creator is necessary, if men are to commit to leaving behind their fixation on ambition, sex, video games, drugs, alcohol and big boy toys.

The story of Bob Chadwick's journey has the gritty feel of reality to it. He is, in a sense, "Every man." His selfishness and self-indulgence may be different from our own, but it demonstrates the high cost we pay for doing things "our way." Bob is a man with deep regrets, painful remorse and significant losses. The brokenness of his life is as real as the blown out knee of an NFL celebrity athlete. The blood and guts familiarity of his failures is what we have all either witnessed in others or experienced ourselves. That's what makes Bob's turn around and recovery in spite of a high degree of difficulty so powerful.

This is not some rare religious emotional or psychological trip. Millions of men have found the same Lord and Savior that Bob did. The story of a man returning to his Creator and finding the love of a patiently waiting Father is not mere religious imagination. It rings as true as any rescue and recovery story from today's headlines. And, it radically alters a man's quality of life and the trajectory of his destiny.

The most important breakthrough in life comes when a person finds out they are valued and loved in spite of the mess they have made of things.

Experiencing God's forgiveness brings a kind of relief that is hard to quantify. It starts something that begins to put life back together again...the way it was meant to be. There is absolutely nothing that compares to the freedom from guilt and shame that faith in Jesus offers. It is a faith that obeys our Creator's design and purpose for our existence. A faith that produces the last thing a rebellious heart deserves or expects: peace with God! What follows such peace is the life long process of becoming an un-self-centered human being in the likeness of our Commander-in-chief, Jesus Christ. And that is not easy.

Bob finds out that he needs a lot of help. He can see that dependence on God is essential to his transformation process. What he doesn't suspect was how important accountability to other people would be in his growth as well.

The adventure in this book is seen in how genuine love works, how important honest committed relationships with others are in the recovery of a healthy thinking and acting pattern. If you are a man in the process of becoming your best self, your safe self, in the pursuit of genuine love, this will be an exciting and satisfying read. It will demand courage and persistence, but finishing it and applying it will be worth your time and effort. As you will discover, "Roothog Island" is out there in the mist for you too.

Let Bob row you out to your own island of recovery from the twisted thinking of a self centered life.

JAN D. HETTINGA
Author of **The Safe King**: Finding in Jesus the Leader You Can Trust,
and **Still Restless**: Conversations That Open the Door to Peace.

1

Bob Chadwick left Sandusky, Ohio, an angry man resenting the close relationship between his wife, Lois, and Sandra, their teenage foster daughter, who had clearly threatened his authority as the man of the house. After months of secret planning, Bob packed a few things in the old Ford, left Lois a note, and drove away from his life.

Nearly a year later, after settling in the tiny village of Ellison Bay in Door County, Wisconsin, Bob realized he couldn't hide from himself. His new friend Van had introduced him to Jesus, giving Bob a good look deep into his soul. It was time to make some changes. He would return to Ohio and try to pick up the broken pieces and rebuild his marriage.

* * *

The five hundred and sixty mile trip from Ellison Bay to Sandusky Bay was too much to do in a day, but it didn't matter. The miles flew by as Bob's focused on the conversations he needed to have with Lois, his thoughts ranging from dread to eager anticipation. He knew he'd been a self-absorbed jerk, which was the Chadwick way. But the thought of learning to love and allowing himself to be loved made him come alive.

Bob left Ellison Bay as a man *on the mend* just beginning to accept the blame for the appalling amount of pain he'd perpetrated in his marriage. His drinking and pornography had caused deep wounds.

He also carried some personal baggage into the marriage after growing up in West Virginia with an abusive father. There was also his paralyzing experience of sexual abuse in the urinal of a West Virginia coal mine that left Bob emotionally vacant and calloused. Then, after the pain of losing Joey, their only son, Bob eventually walked out on his wife.

Right now, all he could think about was getting to Sandusky Bay and asking for Lois's forgiveness.

* * *

As Bob approached Sandusky, he decided to stop for a bit at the Ottawa National Wildlife Refuge. It would be a great place to step out of the Ford and gather his thoughts. The two-lane road into the preserve curved to the west and then crossed open water.

Suddenly, Bob felt a dark shadow move across his left shoulder. Startled, he glanced up in time to see a huge black shape with a white head and a golden...

What the heck! A bald eagle!" he yelled.

The road had no shoulder so he stopped his car to marvel at the sight, blocking the cars behind him. The majestic bird passed just a few feet above him, headed for a marshy area at the edge of the lake.

Bob had never seen a bald eagle in Door County, although the peninsula featured a rugged coastline and several natural areas. His friend Van had told him Door County's early Native Americans believed an Eagle flying overhead was a sign of the

Lake Of Bays

Creator's blessing. Could this be a good sign for him in anticipating his talk with Lois?

Bob wondered if it would be possible to rebuild his marriage. However, he reminded himself the reason for talking this time was to ask her forgiveness, whether the marriage went forward or not. As a new follower of Jesus, he was learning to live a new way.

A few minutes later Bob stopped in at an old bait shop for a soda pop. An enormous ginger tabby cat was sprawled on the counter beside the cash register, eying him lazily as he paid for his drink. Then he quickly exited the shop.

He found a picnic table and sat down to enjoy his soda and think through the days ahead, listening to a symphony of Songbirds overhead. He thought about his friend, Van. He was honored when Van asked him to pray for him. Van had been asked to take a position at the boot camp for 2BRealMen on the Lake of Bays in Ontario, Canada and he needed to make a decision. Bob paused to pray for Van.

"God, I have a lot of things on my mind, as you already know. But my buddy Van needs help in determining what he should do, just like I do. I don't know what to say other than asking you to let Van know if he should take that job. I don't know how you do stuff like that, but would you do it?"

Bob hesitated and then continued, *"I don't know what's ahead for me either, but I want to repair my broken relationships. I know Van is praying for me, too. So God, would you help me know what to say and do when I meet Lois? I also need help knowing what to say to my friend Al. Thank you."*

Bob had no idea how much he would need God's help.

2

Bob finished his soda and was eager to head toward Sandusky Bay and see Lois. He decided the best approach was to be as natural as possible, knowing it would be awkward. In fact, it would be completely understandable if she didn't even want to talk to him.

*   *   *

As he approached the Sandusky city limits, Bob took in the familiar landmarks. He anticipated pulling into the driveway of his home and stepping out onto his own property. Turning into his neighborhood, he waved at a neighbor out in his yard. The homes were small and the streets had no curbs or sidewalks. His house was just a block from the bay and he was glad to be home. Happy memories flooded his mind.

"Man, I love the fresh spring air and the smell of the lake!" he thought. *"Joey and I have caught some good lunkers in that bay!"*

More pleasant memories scrolled through Bob's head. He remembered how Lois kept their home so clean and tidy. He also remembered her good cooking and female touches around the house. She had created a sense of normalcy for their family. It all made Bob long for another chance. *"Just one more turn and three houses down, and I'll see Lois!"*

That's when he saw the *For Sale* sign in front of his house. Bob's good memories dissolved into confusion and dread.

"What's going on?" he asked losing his composure.

Apprehensively, he stepped out of the Ford to check the doors.

"Locked!"

Bob tried his key.

"The locks have been changed?"

Unnerved, he walked around the house, looking into all the windows.

No furniture. Empty.

Even the lock to the shed in the back yard had been changed. He noticed the picnic table was gone as well.

"Everything? Everything is gone!"

All Bob's anticipation melted into anguish. How was he going to find Lois to ask her to forgive him?

"Where is Lois?" he wondered. *"What happened to Sandra, our foster daughter?"*

Bob could barely breathe. He felt like he had just taken a punch to the gut.

"Why is that damned sign in front of my house?" he fumed.

Noticing a phone number on the sign, Bob decided to call the real estate company. He located a phone booth near the local drug store, outside the Sandusky License Bureau. Anxiously, he dialed the number.

"Hello, this is Silvia at the Realtor's Co-op. How may I help you?"

"There's a For Sale sign in front of my house on Ogontz Street and I'd like to know who put it there!" Bob demanded.

"I'm sorry sir. The agency can't release that information over the phone. You'll have to come to the office and speak with one of our agents," Sylvia replied.

Lake Of Bays

"What do you mean you can't release that information?" Bob shouted. "It's my house!"

"Well, sir, we will need to see your identification and we will need the owner's permission to reveal that information."

"I am the owner!" Bob interrupted.

"I'm very sorry, sir, but the agency cannot release private information over the phone."

"We'll see about that!"

Bob, irritated and baffled, slammed the phone down on its cradle. Suddenly he thought about the one person who would be able to answer his questions. He climbed back into the old Ford and headed toward Al's house.

*   *   *

It was early evening by the time Bob parked his car in front of Al's house. Big Al had been Bob's friend and mentor. When he knocked on the door, no one answered at first. Finally, Al's brother, Richard, opened the door.

"Bob!" Richard blurted, surprised to see Bob standing there. "Been a while since we've seen you around here. Come on in."

As he motioned toward a chair in the living room, Richard said, "I thought you moved to Door County!"

Bob looked startled. "Why would you think that?"

"When you were staying here you drooled over the book I showed you about Door County. You took the book and a brochure home with you to study. I remember wondering how long it would take you to get there," Richard said in a manner of fact way. "Then I heard you had abandoned Lois and I figured that's where you went."

Lake Of Bays

Bob was stunned. He hadn't realized he had been so transparent.

"I didn't abandon her," he protested defensively. "I left her the house, my disability checks and some cash."

Richard wasn't buying it. He was about to reply when Al came in from working in the back yard. Seeing Bob standing in his living room completely threw him off balance. The men stared at each other for several moments.

Sensing the tension, Richard decided to leave the two of them alone.

"I need to get a few things done," he said. "See you guys later."

With a nod, Al turned back to Bob. "Why are you here?" he asked. There was no warmth in his voice.

"It's a long story, Al." Bob lowered his head. Al stood waiting, silent.

"When I left Lois, I believed our marriage was over. I moved to Wisconsin to start a new life. I thought if I left her enough money, she and Sandra would be fine. I know it wasn't right." Bob couldn't look at Al but could tell he was deeply troubled. He paused, took a breath and continued.

"While I was in Ellison Bay I met a guy named Van who helped me understand what it means to have a relationship with Jesus. He told me the same things you tried to tell me but I guess I wasn't ready. I began to see what kind of person I've been. You were a real friend to me and I hurt you. I hurt Lois most of all."

Al was looking intently at Bob. He had never heard Bob talk like this. In fact, when Bob disappeared and abandoned Lois, he had written him off. He was still skeptical.

"Are you saying you know Jesus as your Savior?" he asked.

JERRY PRICE & TOM ROY

"This is all new for me, but yes," Bob answered. "That's why I'm here. I want to ask your forgiveness. I've been a jerk. An insensitive, selfish, twisted jerk. I made sure I got satisfaction any way I could. I was only thinking of myself." Bob looked down again.

"I'm asking your forgiveness for being a poor excuse of a man. I've been a lousy friend and I've disrespected you and all the ways you've cared for me over the years. Can you forgive me, Al?"

"Yes, I *can* forgive you, Bob."

Bob felt some relief but realized there was still some distance between them. There was a look of sadness on his old friend's face. He waited for Al to speak.

"You've made this hard on me, Bob." Al began. "I don't think anyone else has hurt me as much as you. I was deeply disappointed and angry with you for the way you left Lois. Truthfully, I gave up on you and tried to get you out of my mind.

I'm not trying to rub your face in anything or condemn you when I say that, but I wanted to be honest with you before I tell you what I'm learning.

God has been dealing with me about being *willing* to forgive you Bob. I never expected to see you again so I thought I could do that. But now here you are, asking. I appreciate you asking me to forgive you and on some level I already have. I've given up holding a grudge against you. I released any bitterness toward you and gave up my desire for revenge. I turned you over to God.

But offering you forgiveness face to face is something else. That's what the Spirit of God has been working on me to do. The reason this is so important is that when I actually say I forgive you, I'm opening a door to continue our relationship."

Lake Of Bays

"To answer your question," Al said, "yes, Bob, I *do* forgive you."

"Does that mean we're still friends?" Bob asked. "Yes, we can be friends, but I'm going to be honest with you. Bob, I love you as a brother and a friend but I don't trust you. It's going to take time. Can you deal with that?"

"I think I can," Bob nodded thoughtfully. "I want to rebuild that trust with you, Al. Whatever it takes."

When there was a natural pause, Al asked Bob if he'd like coffee before they continued the conversation.

"I sure would!" Bob said.

* * *

A few minutes later the coffee was ready. Taking a sip, Al asked Bob if he had anything else on his mind.

"As a matter of fact, I do. I just drove past the house and saw a For Sale sign in front yard! I called the real estate company but they told me they couldn't provide any information over the phone. Do you know what's going on?"

"You haven't heard?" Al asked.

"Heard what?"

Al realized Bob was completely in the dark, which meant he'd have to be the one bearing the bad news. With a heavy heart he looked up, wondering where to begin. Bob was confused when he saw the tears in his friend's eyes.

What's going on, he wondered.

"Bob. Lois is gone."

"What? What do you mean, gone?"

Al took a long breath and continued.

Lake Of Bays

"Shortly after you left, Lois found your note and called me. You said you knew you caused her plenty of pain but she had paid you back with 'Cinderella,' referring to your foster daughter. You left Lois hanging by saying maybe you might be in touch when you landed somewhere.

I asked how she was doing. She said okay, but she kept wondering what you would do without her. I could tell she wasn't okay, so I decided to check in on her every now and then.

A few months passed by and I hadn't seen her, so I stopped by the house Christmas morning. When I knocked on the door there was no answer. I walked around to the back and tried the kitchen door. It was unlocked so I opened the door and called out but didn't hear anything. I decided to step inside and turn on the kitchen light."

Bob sat there, fearing what he was going to hear next.

"That's when I saw her." Al began to weep.

"There was an empty bottle of pills on the kitchen counter. I walked over to check her pulse. There was nothing. She was already gone."

"What are you saying?" Bob was in shock. "Lois is dead?"

Heartbroken, Al said, "Yes."

Bob moaned and slumped in his chair. Slowly a picture was forming in his mind of the incredible pain he had caused Lois over the years. His guilt was greater than he had ever imagined. He didn't know how he could go on. He began to sob.

Learning of the death of his wife was agonizing, but the greatest pain for Bob was the awareness of the pain he had caused her. Now there was no chance for closure. No chance to ask forgiveness. No chance for rebuilding his marriage. Lois was gone!

JERRY PRICE & TOM ROY

Lake Of Bays

"God, what's happening?" Bob's mind was as full of questions as his heart was full of despair. *"I'm so lost. Who am I? What do I do? What do you want from me?"*

"I miss them!" Bob cried out. "I miss Lois. I miss Joey. I miss..." He starts to sob but finishes his thought. "My family!"

Al was silent as Bob sobbed out his grief. Later, he suggested Bob might want to stay at his house that night. There would be time to talk the next day. He knew this was not the time to talk about what lay ahead for him.

3

Bob was in shock. His body and soul numb from the grief. This was different than the grief he had experienced losing his son.

Joey had died from a drowning accident in Canada. As painful as that was, there was some small comfort in knowing Bob and his son had been on track to rebuild their relationship. With Lois it was different.

Grief was magnified by an enormous sense of failure. He had left in anger. Rather than facing her, he left her a note and snuck away like a coward. He was overcome with the guilt of knowing he abused her emotionally.

Bob couldn't imagine her despair. He had been indifferent and arrogant. His drinking and selfishness created a distance in their marriage she wasn't able to overcome. He knew he'd made her feel worthless and discarded which she didn't deserve. He had caused Lois to feel hopeless and then she decided life wasn't worth living. He convulses with grief.

Gradually Bob was becoming aware that in spite of beginning a new life with Jesus, consequences of his past behavior were not going away. He remembered Van telling him, *Bob, the old things are passing away, but they have not passed away. Things are becoming new. Some day when we see Jesus, the old things will pass away for good.*

But for now, Bob knew he had screwed up and needed help.

Lake Of Bays

* * *

Exhausted, Bob dragged himself into the kitchen the next morning where Al was waiting with a fresh cup of coffee.

"Thanks," Bob said, gratefully taking a sip.

"Rough night?" Al asked.

Bob nodded and took another sip. He held back the urge to cry, surprised he had anything left. He knew it would be a tough day.

"Are you ready to talk?" Al asked.

Bob looked down taking a deep breath and blew it out.

"I can't begin to tell you the guilt and shame I feel about how I treated Lois. I came to the conclusion last night that I should feel that way. There is no denying the truth. In my mind I heard her voice for the first time, but it came from her grave. *'Too late!'* she said."

Bob fought back his tears.

Al sat in silence as Bob talked.

"I don't know what to do, or what is the right thing to do, but I think I want to visit her gravesite this morning. After that, would you have some time to talk through what lies ahead for me?"

"Absolutely," Al agreed.

He gave Bob directions to finding where Lois had been laid to rest. He knew it wasn't the right time yet for advice.

With a nod, Bob got up from the table and left.

* * *

JERRY PRICE & TOM ROY

Lake Of Bays

The Sandusky Cemetery on Milan Road was a quiet and beautiful place. The grounds were well kept and the views were stunning. Bob was hoping, needing somehow, to spend time privately with Lois in a spiritual way. That was something new for him.

He found her gravesite and sensed a sacredness as he approached. The morning dew had evaporated and he sat silently for a long time, looking at the headstone. Finally he spoke.

"Lois, I'm sorry," he said, awkwardly. "I was looking forward to having a conversation with you. I realized I wanted to be married to you and returned to Sandusky to see if you would have me. I had some idea of how much I hurt you through the years. But I had no idea how much until I got here yesterday."

The tears Bob had been holding back began to fall.

"I wish I could take it all back and start over. I wish I could learn how to be a real husband and man. I thought I knew everything but the truth is I didn't know anything.

Will you forgive me? Will you forgive me for pushing you away, for not treating you with the honor and respect you deserved, for being a weak man and father to our son? Will you forgive me for being a loud mouth, drunken slob and for paying more attention to my beer and girly magazines than you? Will you forgive me for keeping secrets from you and for walking out on you?"

A deep sense of disgust and self-contempt began to fill Bob's soul. Not knowing how to respond, he began speaking to God. He found himself looking toward the sky, as if he was in a three-way conversation with God and Lois.

"God, I don't know if Lois can hear or forgive me, but will you forgive me?"

Lake Of Bays

"Lois, I remember early in our marriage when you told me about the time you first believed in Jesus. It was at His Word Community Baptist Church and you were a young girl. At the time I could not have cared less. Now my only hope is that I will one day see you again in heaven."

"God, it feels strange to ask you this, but would you tell Lois how sorry I am? Would you also tell her I look forward to seeing her and Joey again someday?

I know I need help, God. I'm not sure what to do. I'm asking that you show me what kind of help I need. Thank you."

A deep sadness accompanied Bob to the Cemetery. That feeling didn't go away, but somehow he left with a glimmer of hope. He never had a conversation with God like that before. For that matter, he never had a conversation like that with Lois either.

The journey toward getting help was just starting for Bob and he knew it. He had some idea where that journey could begin, but first, he needed to have another talk with Al.

It occurred to him that in the depth of his sorrow, hope was beginning to take root. That was a first for Bob. His grief was tangible and hope was tiny, but it felt productive. He didn't understand it all, but wherever he was headed in life, it would be one step at a time.

4

Grief was paralyzing. Bob had no idea what lay ahead for him, but he believed talking with Al would give some direction for his future. He was aware of more personal debris in his life that needed to be cleared. He also assumed there were incidentals, which had to be addressed. And, Bob somehow sensed this might be his last opportunity to have a good talk with Al and he was determined to take in every word.

* * *

Bob was shattered in a way he had never been before. Several times on the drive back to Al's he needed to pull off the road because he simply couldn't see through the flood of tears.

Bob rarely cried. His tough West Virginia background had taught him 'real men don't cry.' In the past, any tears at all had been tears of self-pity. This was different. Bob's tears were coming from a place of genuine sorrow for all the pain he had caused others.

Al could visibly see a difference in Bob when he walked in the door. He knew he was ready to talk.

"Are you ready for another cup of coffee?" he asked. Grateful, Bob poured himself a cup and sat down at the table. They sat in silence for several minutes before Al asked if Bob was okay.

Lake Of Bays

"Yes, I think so." Struggling to find words, he began to tell Al about his conversation with Lois and with God."

"I told them I needed help and asked to be forgiven." Bob felt his eyes filling with tears again. He couldn't speak for a few minutes. Taking a shaky breath, he tried again.

"It's so hard to accept Lois is gone and I'll never have the chance to make up for all the hurt I've caused her. That's what pains me the most.

Yet somehow, in the middle of all that, this strange peace I've never experienced before came over me. I don't remember ever being so clearheaded in my life, even though I have no idea what's ahead. But I believe there is something new ahead for me."

Hearing himself express these thoughts out loud made Bob wonder if he was losing it. "Do you think I'm just stuffing things and avoiding reality because it's too painful? Am I creating my own fantasy world?" he asked Al.

"Hmmm," Al began. "I have a couple of thoughts about all this."

"I'm listening." Bob waited.

"I'm not sure you are stuffing things. Over the last several years you've suffered some major losses. You have lost your dad, your son and your wife. You've had to deal with Rico's betrayal as a pastor and friend. You've suffered a career ending injury and loss of your job at the mill. You suffered the loss of your dream of Joey becoming a major league baseball player. And yes, you've lost the opportunity to rebuild your marriage with Lois. That's a lot to handle, Bob.

I appreciate you realizing you've been a 'jerk,' as you called yourself, but anyone going through all those losses in a relatively short period of time has been grieving for quite a while. You've been grieving more than you realize. Stuffing things? Avoiding reality? I don't think so."

Bob had never considered it that way. As he took in Al's words, he felt the heaviness of all he had been through. In fact, he realized he was carrying a huge weight on his shoulders since his youth. Maybe his unexpected flood of tears had been about much more than he imagined.

"There's something different about the way you're handling things now. What do you think it is?" Al asked.

"I'm not drinking to avoid my problems."

"You're facing them head on, like a man. You're talking more. You're listening more instead of just spouting off." Then, Al said. "I'm proud of you Bob."

Bob was thoughtful. *"Maybe it has something to do with understanding Jesus loves me."*

"Did you know Jesus likes you?" Al asked.

That did it. Just when Bob thought he had no more tears left in him, a dam broke and he couldn't hold it back. What Al had just asked profoundly touched him.

"No one has ever said that to me before. Jesus actually *likes* me!"

It was a completely new thought to Bob. He didn't think anyone really liked him, including himself! Of all people, Jesus liked him enough to want to hang out with him. It was a realization that was both humbling and wonderful. This time his tears came from a place of joy.

After a few moments, Al asked, "Are you ready for another thought?"

Bob answered with new confidence. "Bring it on."

"You've lived your life with a false idea of what it means to be a man. I think you are about ready to turn a corner and learn from men who can help you reshape that. Men who will care for you but they won't put up with your old way of stiff-arming and bullying your way out of accountability. They will respect you as a man and model what it means to genuinely love and respect others."

Bob was listening.

"We learn by watching other men. Unfortunately, the men in your life modeled a selfish and unhealthy way of living. It's time to change that."

"You're right!" Bob exclaims.

Things were beginning to make sense to Bob.

"Al, I've wanted to say this to you before. You're the first man I've ever met who had the guts to tell me the truth without making me feel condemned. I think it's because I know you care about me. It might be hard to hear but deep down I want to hear what you are saying. I feel like I'm still a kid living in a man's body, but I want to know what it feels like to be a man in a man's body."

Al looked Bob in the eye. "This is where I need to step aside for a while, so you can go work on that."

Perplexed, Bob stared and asked, "What are you saying?"

"I'm saying that ever since I've known you when we worked together at the mill, I've been like a dad to you. Am I right?"

Bob thought about it and nodded. He wasn't sure where this was going.

"Even though you are like a son to me, you're more than that. You're a friend and a brother in Christ."

Al let that sink in. "That's the way I want it to be. I'm not your father, Bob. I'm your friend. God is your true Father and I believe he will re-father you."

Lake Of Bays

Al continued. "I think it's time for you to identify with other men outside Sandusky, Ohio. You need to find some men who are brothers in the Lord."

Bob was not expecting this but oddly enough, he fully agreed. Al was right. The truth is there *was* nothing for him in Sandusky Bay any more.

"Wherever you go or whatever you decide to do, I'm a phone call away. I will be praying you grow as a man. That God will open up your heart to experience the wonders of a relationship with Him. Like any good father, he will teach, discipline and challenge you out of love.

I had an old friend, another brother in the Lord, who used to say every time he left, 'See you here, there or in the air.' He knew there was always a chance we would not see each other again in this life, but we will see each other again someday because of Jesus."

Bob knew their friendship would not end when he left Sandusky. Time and distance would not change that. But he was aware of the possibility he might not see his friend again and decided to do something he had never done before.

Quietly, he said, "Al, I love you. Thank you for being a friend to me. You're still like a father to me but I understand what you're saying. There's no father like God the Father."

"Exactly!" Al smiled and embraced his friend.

*   *   *

They talked for over an hour and it was past lunchtime. Deciding to take a break, they went get a sandwich at Mo's Custom Meats.

Lake Of Bays

Bob had met Mo, short for Massimo, a little while before he left town for Ellison Bay, WI. He liked the way Mo called him *Bawb*, since Mo came from New *Yawk*.

Mo was a straight shooter and loved to joke around. He was a man's man and still had a genuine faith in God. Bob would never forget Mo's account of his tragic loss. His wife, Linda, had been alone at the shop cleaning up for the night when she was assaulted and murdered. Al had introduced him to Mo, thinking Mo's story might help Bob work through his own tragedy after Joey drowned.

Mo's had the reputation for the best burgers in town. As they walked through the door, they heard Mo's booming voice.

"Look who we have here! Bet you two are lookin' for burgers and free French fries, huh?"

"You haven't changed a bit," Bob said, warmed by Mo's big personality and unique welcome.

"Haven't seen you around here lately, Bawb. Where you been?"

"Wisconsin. I'm not proud of it, Mo, but I left Lois, like a coward. Instead of fighting for my marriage I was planning to start over. But I met a man in Door County named Van. He was a different kind of guy but he introduced me to Jesus."

"I decided to come home and see if Lois would forgive me and take me back. I hadn't kept in touch so I didn't know about what happened to her."

Mo knew about Lois because he and Al were friends. But he was surprised by Bob's candor. This was not the same guy he had met before.

"I realized what I jerk I really was," Bob continued.

"Well, Bawb, you know I used to be a piece of shit, too, right?" Mo asked with a sideways smile.

Lake Of Bays

"No question, Mo." Bob replied with a nod and his own sideways smile.

"Sounds like you're on the right road. Happy you've met Jesus and sorry about your wife. I know what that's like."

Bob nodded again.

"So what's next for you?" Mo was always direct. "Al and I were just talking about that. There are a few things I need to get settled here in Sandusky, but after that it looks like I'll be heading out of town. Only this time I won't be running from anything. I'll be running toward something that God has for me, even though I don't know yet what that will be."

Al was pleased. It sounded like Bob had embraced the idea of being re-fathered and learning from other men what it means to be a man who follows Jesus.

"Al and I will talk through a few of the details, but not until after we eat the best burger on the planet."

Mo grinned.

"You're always welcome to stop in for another burger, Bawb." Mo was treating Bob like a brother and it felt good.

"Any idea where you will be going?"

"Not real sure right now. But I'm confident God has something in mind. Should be interesting!"

* * *

Back at the house, Bob sat down with Al for what would be one of their last good talks before he left Sandusky.

"I really like Mo," Bob began. "That guy is the best! I love his energy. Just listening to him and how he's dealt with losing his wife has been a huge encouragement to me. Thanks for introducing us."

Lake Of Bays

Al nodded. "You're welcome. Now, is there anything you'd like to talk about? Do you have any ideas about what you want to do next?"

"Yes, but first I want to tell you something I decided when I visited the cemetery. I'm wondering if you could help."

"Okay, I'm listening," Al said.

"I'm not sure what needs to happen with the sale of the house. In fact, I'm not too concerned about it. But here's what I'm thinking. I would like to ask if you would make sure the profit goes to Sandra? I'll take care of any paperwork or legal fees. Would you be willing to follow up?"

Al was completely caught by surprise. The old Bob would have fought for that money and held a grudge against Sandra if she had tried to claim it. This was evidence of a genuine heart change in his friend.

"Sure, Bob. I'll do that. I have to admit, I'm blown away by this." Al shook his head.

"Do you mind if I ask you a question about Sandra?" he asked.

Bob nodded hesitantly.

"Are you planning to see her before you leave town to repair your relationship?"

"No." Bob shook his head. "I wish I could but I'm not sure how well I would handle it. I'm not sure I wouldn't get angry."

Al listened and waited.

"There might be a time in the future I could meet with her if she is open to it, but I'm not ready now. I don't want to act like the asshole she thinks I am. My intent is to let her know through you that the profit from the house is hers. Heck, I'm the one who left it all behind, so in my mind that money is not mine anyway.

Lake Of Bays

"When I was at the cemetery, I told Lois how sorry I was for taking any joy away from her about having a daughter. I'm doing this for Lois." Bob was choking back his emotion. "Do you think that's okay?"

"Yes." Al nodded. "When you feel ready to talk with Sandra, I know you will do it. So I'm okay with it."

Bob valued his friend's opinion.

"Is there anything else on your mind?"

"Yes, actually, there is. I'd like to call my friend Van to see if he's taken that ministry job in Canada. If he has, I'm going ask if he thinks I might be a candidate for one of their boot camp guys who come to get help. If they accept me, that's where I'm headed."

Al nodded his approval.

"I have another favor to ask. May I stay with you until I get that all set up? It might take a while. I'm not sure how it works."

"You truly are on a new journey, my friend." Al smiled. "I'm very happy for you and I'll be praying God opens this door. Until you head out, you're welcome here and I'll support you anyway I can."

5

The next few days were spent at Al's house resting. Finally, Bob called Van, his Door County friend. But he found himself in low spirits as he dialed the number. Not being sure as to why.

The phone rang several times before his friend picked up the phone. "Sea Port Potty Service, how may I help you?"

"Van? It's me."

"Bob? Where are you? What's going on with you?" Van asked.

Bob related the story he faced after returning to Sandusky. The news rocked Van. He knew about Bob's desire to reconcile with Lois and he was shocked to hear of the suicide.

"Oh, my friend! I'm sad for you. This is hard!"

"Thank you, Van." Bob paused to gain his composure. "If you hadn't introduced me to Jesus before I left Ellison Bay, I don't know if I would have believed anything was worth living for. As it is now, I'm a mess."

"I hear you. You've got to be crushed by what's happened. I can't imagine what's going on inside of you."

That broke the dam again, and Bob couldn't hold it together. Van knew him pretty well. He knew Bob was the type of guy who'd work to put up a good front and act like he had everything under control. He would present his confident side, no matter what. Van used to tell him something that put things in perspective. *Bob, we're all made of the same mud.*

Bob knew Van saw through him. He had put a finger on just how crushed he really was.

"Van, could I call you back?"

"You bet, buddy. Take your time. I'll be available."

Lake Of Bays

* * *

Loneliness is different than aloneness. Aloneness is separation from others and is not necessarily an unhappy experience. Loneliness is experienced as a sense of isolation or lack of companionship, even when surrounded by others.

Bob had experienced both during his lifetime. His current situation of aloneness was undeniably an unhappy experience. He desperately missed Lois.

He couldn't put his finger on it but Bob was slowly becoming aware that his emotional divorce from Lois not being caused by their foster daughter. Feeling weird, he was unable to manage his shame. His emotions were out of control. It was crazy how one word, like *crushed*, unlocked all of this in him.

Bob used to think he had it all figured out. He thought he was in control of his life and when he had problems it was someone else's fault. Unpredictably, the script of his life was being rewritten and he knew his whole life had been a lie.

The truth hit him hard when he heard the concern in Van's words. Yes, he was crushed, but the truth is he was the one who crushed others his whole life, especially his wife. He found himself owning that and it hurt, which was why he had to ask Van if he could call him back. It was a lot to process.

Ten minutes later, Bob thought, *I need to call Van back and be totally up front about letting him know I really need help.*

* * *

"Sea Port Potty Services. How may I help you?"
"Van, it's Bob again."

JERRY PRICE & TOM ROY

"You okay, Bob?"

"Yes. Well, truthfully, no. I need to talk with you.
I'm sorry for hanging up like that."

"No problem, my friend. I know you've been through a lot so I didn't think anything of it. Tell me what's going on. How can I help?

"You said something that hit me hard and I had to sort it out."

"What did I say?" Van asked.

"You said something about how I must be crushed. It's true, I am absolutely crushed by all this, but when you said it, all I could think about was how I'm the one who did the crushing. I'm the reason my marriage fell apart. I'm the reason my wife fell apart and killed herself. I crushed Lois, Van!"

"It's tough putting those thoughts together," Bob continued. "I miss Lois. But I'm realizing I'm responsible for the mess I'm in.

"How did you sort it out?" Van asked.

"The only thing I can think of is to be completely honest with you. I need to lay some stuff on the table," Bob answered.

"Go for it!"

"I need help, Van. Things have happened so fast since I returned to Sandusky. What you taught me in Door County has helped me admit some of my failures and also experience some forgiveness from God. But I keep hitting snags. I just don't know enough about God or about the Bible and I think I need help with that."

"I hear what you're saying," Van encouraged. "But think about this. If just having knowledge of God and an understanding of the Bible as the requirement to avoid those snags, a lot of people would be up a creek. Think of the people who can't read. Think of the people who don't have access to a Bible."

"I never thought of it that way," Bob said.

"Very few people have ever seen Jesus face to face, since he was only on earth for thirty three years. But that doesn't mean we can't know Jesus." Van added. "So, do you know what God does?"

"I'm all ears," Bob said.

"He puts us into relationships with other people who love Jesus who have come to know him well, even though they've never actually seen him. People who have an understanding of the Bible and are able to teach or preach or model what it means to walk by faith.

No believer is an island unto himself, Bob. Even God the Father is not alone. He's a Trinity with the Son and the Holy Spirit. And in that trinity, they never isolate themselves from each other. They work in unity."

Bob listened to Van attentively.

"They have an agreement between them to work through humans to introduce others to Jesus, after people have embraced the metaphorical womb of God, to help them grow up in their faith."

"You lost me there, Van. Would you dumb it down a bit? Especially that part about the metaphorical womb of God."

"Sure," Van agreed. "Remember when Jesus told Nicodemus that he must be born again?"

"Yes. You used to hammer me with that during our earlier talks in Ellison Bay."

"That's right! I believe Jesus was saying something like this: *'Nick, you're a big shot teacher in the Jewish ruling body but as hard as you worked at achieving and keeping that position, it doesn't get you into heaven. You're going to have to start over and when you do, you start with me. So you're right, I'm not talking about a physical rebirth. I'm talking about something that happens inside of you Nick. Something that will guarantee you a home in heaven.'*

"I did that when I was with you in Door County, right?" Bob asked.

"I was simply the human God used to bring you to this truth. You never heard me say you have to start your life over with me, did you?"

"True, I didn't." Bob said.

"We each need to start a new life with Jesus! It doesn't matter if we are rich or poor, young or old, religious or not. It's the same for everyone, the doctor, the factory worker, the teacher, the janitor, the pro athlete, the politician, the criminal or even the shit house captain! We're all made of the same mud.

Being born again means starting over with Jesus. God the Father loves us and draws us to Jesus. God the Spirit chooses to live inside us to teach us about him. That's what I mean by embracing the metaphorical womb of God.

It's like we're inside of God's womb, totally dependent on him for living life."

"Okay, I understand but how does this apply to me about needing help?" Bob asked.

"I know I'm taking the long way around to answer your question," Van chuckled. "But remember, I am a bible teacher. That's what my job will be when I move to Canada."

"You took that job!" Bob excitedly responds. "I've prayed for you about that decision, like you asked."

"Thank you, Bob! I really appreciate that. I'll be teaching at a place called Roothog Island in Lake of Bays, Ontario. It's a boot camp for men. There are five men on staff and they only accept one man at a time so that man gets their undivided attention. The goal? Help each man who attends the boot camp to become the man God built him to be.

To answer your question, Bob, here's what I'd like to suggest. I'm willing to ask the staff if they'd consider accepting you to the boot camp. Are you interested?"

"That's exactly what I need!" Bob said. "I've been talking with my friend, Al. As a mentor, he said he can only go so far with me and then encouraged me to find a place where I can be re-fathered. He thought it would be good to find a group of men who wouldn't be intimidated by my attitudes. Do you think they would accept me?"

"I think there's a good chance," Van replied. "If they do, there's something I want you to keep in mind. Even though we're human, this group is a part of God's team. When you were in Ellison Bay, you started your life over with Jesus. But as you grow, it will feel like you are starting over in quite a few ways. There will be some Bible study and along with that, a lot of relationship work. Being re-fathered is a good way to put it.

Bob, it's great that you realize you need help and are interested in understanding the Bible. As I said, none of us can do this alone, my friend."

"I think I'm learning that," Bob said.

"You should know your accountability team on Roothog Island is totally involved in the process. Every part of your life will be under scrutiny; what you believe, how you think, the way you make decisions and how those choices affect others. Everything, Bob, including your habits and behaviors, will be examined. It will be hard-hitting but also respectful and loving. Does this still sound like something you'd like to do?"

"Yes!" Bob said, sincerely.

Lake Of Bays

"There's one more thing, Bob. The program on Roothog Island is called 2BRealMen for Christ and it's a brand new ministry. We have some donors who'll help cover some of the cost of operations, but we ask the men who come to boot camp to put some skin in the game. You will be required to cover some of your expenses on the island. It's a twelve to twenty-four week process, depending on how much time you need. Are you okay with that?"

"Absolutely," Bob agreed.

"Okay, I'll be in touch. I'll be leaving Door County in about a month. Meanwhile, I'll contact the other men on the island and make sure they all agree. Once I get their okay, I'll let you know and we can go from there."

"Sounds good, Van. Thank you for considering me. I'll wait to hear from you."

* * *

Bob's sense of aloneness and loneliness began to lift. Even though there was a degree of uncertainty about being accepted into the program and staying on an island with a crazy name like Roothog, it felt good to have *truth* as a new friend in his life.

Excited, Bob could hardly contain himself to let Al know.

6

When Al heard Bob was a possible candidate for the accountability program that his friend had mentioned, he was pleased. He hoped it would work out for Bob and let him know he was welcome to stay until he learned about the boot camp decision.

This time living at Al's house was a bit more awkward than the last visit. The first time Bob stayed there, Al's younger brother, Richard, was living with Al but Bob was so preoccupied with his own issues, he hadn't paid much attention to anyone else.

His marriage had been in crisis. Lois was convalescing in the hospital after overdosing on pills. He was dealing with his own alcohol abuse and staying with Al until he figured out what do next. Richard had been friendly but kept to himself while Bob spent most of his time with Al.

This time Richard seemed more like a wife than a brother! Occasionally Bob observed them hugging each other! Bob was from coal mining country and was not accustomed to men showing affection. For now, however, he avoided questions about their relationship, *I'm not here to rock their boat,* he thought.

* * *

Five weeks had passed since Bob's return to Sandusky Bay. It was now mid-October and the fall colors were vivid. It had been a month since he last heard from Van. Al's telephone began ringing and Bob was the only one home.

"Hello, Al's residence. This is Bob speaking. May I help you?"

"Bob, it's Van!"

"Hey, Van. Good to hear your voice!"

"I know you've been waiting to hear from me about the decision from the 2BRealMen guys," Van said. "I'll keep it short but brace yourself."

That doesn't sound good, Bob thought. *Brace yourself?* Bob was full of uncertainty and apprehension. He had been waiting for Van to call, hopeful about being accepted into the program but fearful at the same time. It was only a few seconds before Van continued but it seemed like a lifetime.

"You've been accepted by 2BeRealMen boot camp on the Lake of Bays," Van announced. "Two weeks from now you will be full-bore into the accountability process."

"Yes!" Bob shouted. He was both relieved and excited. "This is great news!"

He could hear Van laughing on the phone, sharing the joy. He knew there would be hard work ahead for Bob but the results would be worth it.

Bob hadn't realized just how much he wanted to hear he'd been accepted. He felt like he had just been drafted into professional baseball! A new sense of hope was rising inside him and for the first time in a long time, he looked forward to the future.

Van's voice broke in on Bob's enthusiasm. "Would you like to hear how you were chosen?"

Chosen. That word had such a welcoming sound to Bob.

"Yes, I would!" Bob was eager to hear.

Lake Of Bays

"The team decided you could work your fee off while you go through the treatment. In fact, your work will become a big part of your treatment responsibility on Roothog Island."

This pleased Bob.

"Each man who enters this process is required to sign a contract with his wife or another important person in his life, along with the 2BeRealMen team," Van explained.

"No one goes through this program unless he's at the end of his rope and has betrayed those close to him by committing unconscionable offenses. If he fails to honor the contract he has plenty to lose. That might be his wife, family, career, reputation or wealth."

I've already lost everything! Bob thought.

"As I mentioned, each individual is charged a fee to cover the cost of their treatment process as well as their expenses while staying on the island." Van continued.

"In your case, Bob, we believe you've already lost plenty. The team took this into account, along with the fact that you asked for help. Most of the men who enter the program haven't done that. 'Uncle Joe,' our lead counselor, believes 2BeRealMen is about learning to move responsibly into mystery, which you will understand better as you get into the program. We also want you to know a scholarship has been provided for you to come to Roothog."

Bob was flabbergasted. "I don't know what to say! Thank you! Thank you to the whole team!"

"I'm happy for you, my friend." Van sounded truly pleased. "Pack plenty of warm clothes. Winter is coming and you'll need them."

Lake Of Bays

With a small chuckle, Van added, "Working on Captain Kurt's fishing boat set you up pretty well for the Canadian winter!"

Recalling the bitter cold days of commercial fishing in Wisconsin, Bob said, "Thanks for the heads up!"

"I'll be sending you directions to the Lake Of Bays and how to get to Roothog Island. See you in a couple of weeks!"

Bob thought of several questions but Van hung up before he had a chance to ask. Bob smiled, thinking *I guess that's the beginning of my mystery.*

* * *

It was late evening when Al walked through the front door with Richard. Bob was waiting, excited to relate the news to his friend.

"I've been accepted into the program by the team in Canada!" he blurted. "I'll be heading up there in about a week and a half."

Both Al and Richard expressed their happiness for Bob, but he sensed something else behind their kind words. He looked at Al's face for a clue. There was an awkward silence but Bob waited.

Al cleared his throat. "I have something to tell you, Bob. If you don't mind I like to go wash up first. I'll need about fifteen minutes. Do you have time to talk after that?"

"Sure," Bob curiously responds.

Once the three of them had gathered in the living room, Al took a deep breath and began.

"What I want to tell you isn't about you; it's about me. But first I want to tell you how happy I am for you and how proud I am that you returned to Sandusky to try to make things right with Lois. I'm impressed with how you've handled your life since you learned about her death. I know it was difficult for you to visit the cemetery, but it helped you face some tough things. You've come a long way."

Bob wasn't expecting that but nodded in appreciation. He wasn't sure where the conversation was headed but listened closely to everything Al said.

"I'm elated that Jesus is in your life. You've had your share of sadness and my prayer for you has been that God would lead you in a new direction. You are becoming a man who genuinely cares about others, and that comes from a new mind and heart that only Jesus can give."

Bob glanced over at Richard who was sitting quietly. Bob wondered where he fit in all this, but he continued to listen attentively.

"There's no easy way to say this. When you leave for Canada you will probably be there for several months. When you finish the program you will need to decide where you will go next. If you decide to return to Sandusky there is a pretty good chance I won't be here."

"What are you talking about?" Bob asked.

"I've been seeing an oncologist after having physical problems and went in for some tests. The results showed I have Prostate Cancer. It was stage four so I've been going through a variety of different treatments. But the cancer has spread to other organs and penetrated the bones. The oncologist told me today I have about three months."

"I had no idea!" Bob was stunned. "The boot camp can wait. I want to be here with you. Your friendship means the world to me, Al. I won't leave you!" Bob began to weep for his friend.

"I had a feeling you would say that and it means a lot to me. But my mind is made up. Richard has been here for several months taking care of me. This has brought us closer together as brothers and I'm comfortable with him as my caretaker. I just want you to know how much joy it has given me to see you begin a new journey that God has designed for you."

Suddenly Bob noticed the age and weariness on his friend's face.

"You...you've been like a father to me," Bob stammered. "I love you, Al! I'm going to miss you!"

"And you're like a son to me. Sort of a prodigal son," Al added, smiling. "I wasn't sure you'd ever get your life together! But God is a big God and it's great to be alive when we know God is in control!"

"Bob, I'd like you to promise me one thing. I want you to go to Roothog Island and learn from men who care about you as much as I do. When it gets tough, I want you to promise not to bail. Then one day we'll see Jesus and we will party together!"

Bob shook his head. He wasn't sure he could promise what his friend was asking when Al broke into his thoughts.

"Will you promise me?" he asked pointedly.

Bob knew he was trapped but there was no way he would disappoint Al.

"Yes, my friend. I promise."

The three men sat quietly together, each taking in the weight of the moment. There was sadness, but the tears were about more than sadness. There was a mission to fulfill, a call requiring authenticity and intimacy between men. There was also hope beneath the sadness that came with the expectancy of seeing each other again someday. In heaven!

Lake Of Bays

In the days before leaving for Canada, Bob experienced a sense of belonging like nothing he had known before.

7

Bob received the directions Van mailed him just in time before leaving Sandusky Bay for Canada. By ten o'clock the next morning he was ready to leave. He wasn't looking forward to saying goodbye to Al. He decided, instead, to tell him *So Long*. In his mind that kept the door open to meeting again.

The old Bob would have given Al a stiff-armed handshake, but not anymore. He wrapped his friend in a huge bear hug and Al gladly responded. He knew that Bob's man hug was another step in his growth.

Al kept the so long simple. Like a dad who is confident knowing his son will be just fine, he urged Bob to get going.

"Go on now, boy," he said, smiling. "Get out of here!"

Al and his brother waved as Bob climbed into the Ford. Flashing a big smile, Al added his favorite saying. "See you here, there or in the air!"

Bob smiled affectionately at his old friend and waved back. And without looking back, he turned the Ford toward his new destination, a place called Roothog Island on the Lake of Bays in Ontario, Canada.

He had come a long way since his days as an arrogant, foul mouthed, hardheaded, hard drinking jerk! Now a follower of Jesus, Bob would be the first to acknowledge he had a long way to go to becoming real as a man. Spending time in the 2BeRealMen boot camp was a step in the right direction.

* * *

Lake Of Bays

Driving east toward Cleveland, Ohio, on highway 2, Bob knew if he pushed he could reach the Lake Of Bays in about eleven hours. But he decided to break the trip into two days to give him time for sorting out his emotions.

So much has happened since I left Sandusky Bay the last time! Bob thought. When Bob left Lois he was angry. He was a take-charge kind of guy and he just wanted to get away and start over in Door County. It was far enough away and seemed like another world.

But he was learning that a guy couldn't go far enough to get away from himself. That's when he met Van and eventually realized his life would be a whole lot better if he asked God to take control.

Driving away from Sandusky this time was different. Bob was leaving a place he had lived for almost twenty years. So much history! This time, rather than running away, he was moving toward something. He would be learning to redefine his manhood by moving into an unknown situation, a boot camp, where he would not be in charge. In fact, he knew it would be like living in a fishbowl.

In spite of the growth in Bob's life in recent months, it suddenly hit him that he was heading into a place where he would have *no* control. Panic gripped him! He recognized it as something he still feared, a lot. *How twisted is that*? Bob thought. Maybe, in the back of his mind, he had thought he could manage what would happen on that island with the weird name.

Bob tried to shake off the apprehension. He focused on the road as he passed Vermilion and then Lorain, Ohio. It was a mental battle against fear. Searching for something to think about, he recalled a conversation with Al shortly before leaving.

Lake Of Bays

"I would like to share with you something God has taught me," Al had begun, "about how he moves in my life. Would you like to hear it?"

Knowing he was about to learn something valuable, Bob eagerly said, "I'd love to!"

"I don't want to contradict anything you will be learning while you are at the boot camp in Canada, but this is something I've found helpful. Sometimes the things we should have done in life can haunt us more than the things we shouldn't have done."

"A simple hug or 'I love you,' even taking out the garbage are small things that mean a lot but can be easily neglected."

"Taking out the garbage?" Bob echoed.

"Taking out the garbage without an attitude!" Al responded, with a firm nod.

"When God stirs my heart toward his destiny for my life, he begins by moving in the mundane. I'm not going to try to explain that but I'd like you to remember it whenever you think of me and think about what it might mean in your life. Consider it my gift to you.

"Thank you, Al. I will," Bob said.

* * *

Another two hours to Buffalo, New York! Bob thought.

The miles had flown by, especially as his mind recalled conversations with his friend. Seeing God move in the mundane. Bob turned the phrase over in his mind. Somehow it had settled his fear of the unknown. He had a hunch it would play out someway on Roothog Island.

He'd been on the road for five hours and since he wasn't in a hurry he looked for a motel.

JERRY PRICE & TOM ROY

Lake Of Bays

If God moves in the mundane, whatever that means, Bob thought, *I want to watch for that. I want to learn what they mean by becoming a real man.*

Smiling, he remembered the bear hug when he left. *Well, I'm glad I did that. It won't haunt me tonight that I neglected to hug Al before leaving. I miss him already,* Bob thought, with a stab of pain.

8

After a good night's sleep in a downtown Buffalo motel, Bob enjoyed a 'light' breakfast of juice, biscuits and gravy, followed by a cup of steaming black coffee.

It reminded him of the Viking restaurant in Ellison Bay, Wisconsin. He remembered the burnt offerings that sometimes greeted him at the Viking and he chuckled, thinking about it. Bob missed the group of guys who met there each morning. They poked fun at each other and their laughter was a great way to start the day.

Humor had not been part of his childhood in Coaltown, West Virginia. There had been the occasional barn dance with music to brighten the gloominess of the coalmining town, but Bob couldn't remember any occasions of good natured humor among the men like he had witnessed in Door County. His favorite memory was about visiting the *Lily Bay Social Club* near Sturgeon Bay. It was a small building behind the Lily Bay Sawmill, with low ceilings, a wood stove and sawdust on every surface. The room was full of warmth, guy food and laughter. Upended logs served as chairs and Ralph, the owner, made everyone feel welcome.

Draining the last of his coffee, Bob's thoughts turned to the men on Roothog Island. He wondered what they'd be like. He knew he would be accountable to them, but would there be any humor on the island? Would there be any laughter? Or would it be entirely serious during his stay?

Lake Of Bays

It's okay to ask questions, Bob thought. He had come to value relationships with men who could laugh with each other and laugh at themselves.

His ability to laugh at himself and be okay with it had been missing in Bob's life. And laughter was completely missing in his relationship with his wife. *That was my fault,* Bob admitted to himself.

* * *

The agent at the border security booth was a large man in a black uniform with a patch on his sleeve that said Canadian Border Service Agency. A side handle baton was attached to his leather belt. The man had an imposing presence as Bob smiled and rolled down the window on a bright morning. Wearing his favorite sunglasses, he was relaxed knowing American citizens were allowed to visit Canada for up to six months without a tourist visa.

Since Bob wouldn't be looking for a job or receiving government services, he knew there wouldn't be any problems. However, just in case there might be, Van had sent documents stating the purpose of his visit.

"Good Morning, Sir. May I please see your identification?" The agent asked with a strong, commanding voice.

Bob reached for his driver's license and handed it to the agent.

"I see you are an American citizen, Mr. Chadwick."

"Yes, I am." Bob answered, respectfully.

"What is your reason for visiting Canada, Mr. Chadwick?"

"I'm here to visit a friend." Bob answered, deciding not to offer any more information than necessary.

Lake Of Bays

"Please remove your sunglasses." The agent looked at Bob closely and then down at his driver's license.

"How long are you planning to stay in Canada, Mr. Chadwick?

"I'm not sure," Bob answered, "but not longer than six months."

"Will you be doing anything other than visiting your friend? the agent questioned.

Bob hesitated. "My friend is a Bible teacher at a men's ministry camp on the Lake Of Bays. I will be meeting with him for Bible Study, along with a few other men."

"What is the name of the camp?" the agent asked, looking intrigued.

"2BeRealMen," Bob answered.

The agent looked at Bob intently. "Did you say 2BeRealMen?"

"That's right," Bob answered, feeling uneasy.

"Other than Bible class, what are the meetings about?" the man asked.

"I'm not really sure," Bob truthfully answered.

Not knowing what else to do, he began to tell the man about the recent loss of both his wife and son, and how he had been invited to the camp to recover from his loss and discover what it meant to be a real man.

The officer seemed riveted by Bob's story but aware cars were backing up at the port of entry he said, "Sorry for your loss, Mr. Chadwick. Enjoy your stay in Canada."

He waved Bob forward. The Niagara River flowed beneath him as he crossed the Peace Bridge connecting the US to Canada.

Lake Of Bays

Merging onto Queen Elizabeth Way, Bob realized the border agent had never asked for the documents. Relieved, to be across the border, he focused on the drive.

* * *

Two hundred and forty-two miles to go. Bob would arrive at the Lake Of Bays in a little over five hours, between four and five in the afternoon. He wanted to take a detour to see Toronto's new CN Tower the world's tallest freestanding structure, erected April 2, 1975. But Bob was focused on Lake of Bays and didn't even want to stop for a bathroom break. All his thoughts were about what could be waiting for him on Roothog Island.

9

Passing the turnoff for Toronto, Bob felt a surge of adrenalin. According to the map he knew it was only a hundred and fifty five miles to the Lake of Bays! So, he decided to stop for a quick lunch in Barrie, Canada, before tackling the last leg of the trip. He was truly excited to get started on this new adventure.

As Bob drove up Highway 11, a thought began to take root in his mind. *I'm taking control of my life by giving up control of my life. Hmmm. I'm going into an unknown and taking risks with no guaranteed results.* It seemed contradictory but it made sense to him and he recognized that as the sign of a major shift in his approach to life.

His mind begins to drift toward baseball. *Why am I so obsessed with Major League baseball?* Bob wondered. He thought about the 1975 World Series between the Boston Red Sox and the Cincinnati Reds, which the Reds had won four games to three. Bob had been locked in on the series even though he was a lifelong Giants fan. He clearly remembered his Giants sweeping the Cleveland Indians in the 1954 series; the year his son Joey was born. *Unforgettable!*

Maybe baseball reminded him of his son, who had signed with the Chicago White Sox right after his high school graduation. They chose to celebrate Joey's signing with a fishing trip to Lake Weslemkoon in Canada, which had ended tragically, with Joey drowning in the lake. *I can't let my mind go down this road,* Bob told himself.

Lake Of Bays

However, the thought hit him that baseball was kind of an analogy for his life.

Watching a Major League baseball game was pure pleasure for Bob. He loved the sharp white chalk lines delineating the infield, the foul lines, the batters' box and the on deck circle. The pristine grass would be perfectly cut, probably in a diamond pattern, and the dirt would be perfectly groomed, raked to an impeccable smoothness. It would be raked again during the seventh inning stretch to maintain the perfection of the infield.

He loved the preciseness of umpires when making their calls. He loved the organ, which pumped up the crowds. He loved the habits and routines of the players as they came up to bat or took the pitcher's mound. He loved the way the uniforms looked. He even loved the way the players spit in the dirt! It was an art! Everything was clear-cut and predictable.

That was it! The thought hit him right between the eyes. *Baseball was designed to be predictable!*

Sure, there was drama involved every time someone struck out or hit a home run. Errors, missed calls and injuries all added to the drama of the game. But there were rules and rules made the game predictable. One team would win and one team would lose. That was baseball.

After a few moments Bob came to the following conclusion: *The game wasn't setup to be anything less than perfect, predictable and manageable. And oh, the glory when things were done right and the favorite team won!*

As he thought about his analogy, Bob began to connect the dots with how baseball was a pretty accurate picture of his life.

I was like this! Anything I thought wasn't perfect, predictable or manageable gave me an excuse to get angry or to

Lake Of Bays

nurse my wounds by getting drunk or sneaking out to the shed to lose myself in those damn magazines! And it was all because things weren't going the way I thought they should.

When Bob came to this understanding it floored him. Smacking him in the face, the pain he caused his wife and son by the way he had conducted his life overcame him.

In remorse, he called out to God. *"I hope you can do something with me because I don't know what to do with myself!"*

* * *

After passing Lake Muskoka, Bob drove through Huntsville, Ontario, about ten miles from the Lake Of Bays. Fifteen minutes later after making a right turn off the South Portage Road unto Jo Lee Point Road, he saw the water. The road faded into a two track leading to the lake, where there was a rowboat moored in shallow water. Bob's instructions would be inside that boat.

Spotting the rowboat, he parked the car, taking in the beauty of the lake and Bob's mood lifted. He could sense the serenity in this place, far from the rush of the world around it. From every angle he could see bays and islands forested with trees clad in their fall colors, proudly standing out against the dark evergreens. Every island was beautiful except one. Roothog Island.

* * *

The Lake Of Bays was known as *Canada's playground,* and certainly that's the way it was on Bigwin Island. In the early forties, the Bigwin Inn was a favorite hangout for Hollywood stars as well as dignitaries like the Rockefellers and Canadian Prime Ministers. However, by 1948, economic conditions and changing vacation patterns conspired against any efforts to restore the inn.

Only now, in the seventies, was there an interest in reviving the Bigwin Island Inn.

Yet, for the sportsman, it had never lost the reputation for being the location of the largest trout ever caught off an island shore. A fifty pounder!

A mile south of Bigwin was Fairview Island. This 20-acre triangle shaped island is considered a great natural resource, forested with mature conifers and hardwoods. From 1944 to 1972, Fairview Island hosted an Inter Varsity Christian Fellowship Campus that was used to train missionaries. But in 1972, the island was sold to Dr. Walton Langford and his wife, Helen, and their five children, as a personal family retreat.

A half-mile from Fairview's southern shore was Roothog Island. No one considered it to be worth much. People used to say that nothing good could come out of Roothog.

Unlike Fairview Island, the pine trees on Roothog Island were gnarly and unattractive, with tangled roots that make the island almost uninhabitable. Clearing the island would be far too expensive. In fact, the Canadian Ministry of Natural Resources and Forestry had declared the island had no natural resources that would be useful or beneficial to the surrounding communities.

Roothog Island had existed, uninhabited, until the 2BRealMen Ministry was allowed to purchase the property through an Ontario Crown Land decision in 1973. Their goal was to turn the island into a boot camp for men whose lives were a shipwreck.

Lake Of Bays

The founder of the ministry was a Canadian everyone called Uncle Joe Hope. It was his vision to begin a radical therapeutic approach to transforming men's thinking while caring for their hearts with solid Bible teaching. The ministry focuses on developing a man's character in the context of a substantive accountability system, supported by the relational integrity that involves a team of men, working with one man at a time, for a period of three to six months.

* * *

Lake Of Bays reminded Bob of Door County, Wisconsin. But the islands in the Lake Of Bays were much closer to each other and more approachable than those in Lake Michigan. Bob could see several large islands from where he stood, less than one mile from each other.

He pulled his gear out of the car, locked it and headed for the boat, eager to read his instructions and be on his way to Roothog Island. What he didn't know was that once the lake became frozen, usually in the early winter, he'd be able to walk to his car. For now, he was ready to row!

It was after four in the afternoon and already getting dark, when Bob got into the boat. Heavy clouds were gathering and it looked like he'd be in for some wet weather. Normally when weather patterns moved through the Lake of Bays they would bring light rain, not much more. That's one of the reasons the area was known as the playground of Canada.

Bob wasn't concerned. He had worked on Lake Michigan as a commercial fisherman and wasn't worried about a little rain. However, Captain Kurt's boat was powered by a motor and quite a bit larger. The rowboat would be powered by Bob.

Lake Of Bays

His task? Row a mile and a half to the east side of Roothog Island and dock the boat. There wasn't much gear to load into the craft except for Bob's fishing gear, winter clothes, and a few personal items.

"Lord, give me the strength to do this." Bob threw up a quick prayer as he eyed the darkening sky. *Maybe I can make it to the island before the worst of this hits,* he thought. Then, he pulled a parka out of his duffle bag and shoved off.

* * *

The wind was picking up and there were whitecaps on the lake with no time to rest. *I don't understand why I have to row myself out to the island? This is crazy!* He thought.

When Bob's arms grew tired and he'd let up on the oars for a moment, the distance he had gained would be lost. The frigid water splashed over the sides of the boat, soaking his gear. He hadn't done much physical work in a while and wasn't in the best shape to take on a challenge like this. His muscles ached and his hands were growing numb, but Bob kept rowing.

About thirty minutes into the trip, progress had been made and Bob was approaching the southern tip of the island with a half mile to row. That's when he heard the thunder and reached for his parka.

When the rain came, it came hard and fast. The wind whipped the lake into rugged waves and Bob found himself rowing into the wind. He thought he was up for the challenge but it was much tougher than he had imagined. The wind kept pushing the boat off course.

Great! He thought, angrily. *What a way to start!*

But the storm doused his anger.

JERRY PRICE & TOM ROY

Lake Of Bays

Well, if I have to be stuck in this rowboat, at least there are no sharks in this lake! Bob laughed at his feeble attempt at humor.

Leaning into the task, he pulled the oars until his muscles screamed. His hands were popsicles. Turning to see how far he still had to go, he spotted the wooden dock!

When Bob got closer he could see it was newly constructed. Nearby was a two-story lodge with a porch off the second floor that extended out over the dock, offering some protection. He could smell the smoke from a wood fire coming out of the chimney.

I made it! Bob thought. He couldn't wait to sit by that fire and warm up. No one came out to meet him on the dock but Bob could see the guys through the window. It was almost five thirty and they were inside eating supper. They were dry and warm. He was wet and cold. No problem. He would be joining them in a moment.

10

With the rowboat tied securely to the dock, Bob salvaged his gear and was just stepping out of the boat when a loud crack of thunder nearly knocked him into the lake. It was as if the storm was mocking him, saying, "Welcome to Roothog Island, Big Fella! Get a little wet, aye? Well guess what? That's just the beginning."

Looking toward the thundercloud, Bob nodded and grinned. *"That's all you got? Bring it on!"* he said, under his breath. Although every muscle in his body ached with exhaustion, nothing could dampen his excitement to finally be on Roothog Island and meeting the 2BRealMen team. Let the work begin!

* * *

Bob didn't know what to expect but he knew he was hungry. He couldn't help thinking about supper at the Viking in Ellison Bay, Wisconsin and wondered about the kind of chow he'd be eating for the next few months.

Without knocking, Bob opened the door and hoisted his gear inside. Five men were sitting around a table, talking and eating. The aroma of pan fried lake trout filled the room. He could see mounds of mashed potatoes and green beans. Then he spotted a pot of fresh coffee and a chocolate cake on the counter. As Bob stood there dripping, he asked cheerfully, "Who's the chef? Something smells really good and it's not me!"

Lake Of Bays

Van came over to give Bob a hug and a few slaps on the back.

"You made it! Good to see you, my friend."

"It's good to be here," and Bob meant it.

Van took a step back. "You're wet! And you're right! You do stink!"

They both laughed and then, the other men stood to introduce themselves.

"Hi Bob. Glad you weathered the storm," an older man spoke first. "I'm Joe Hope, but most people call me Uncle Joe. I'm the founder and director of this ship. I'm also the primary counselor and facilitator for your treatment."

Joe noticed Bob's grin. "Let me guess. You're smiling at my name, right?"

Bob said, "Yes, I am. Sorry."

"No problem," Joe said. "At least it's better than Bob Hope." There was a comfortable laughter in the room.

Then a man Bob guessed to be about six feet five inches tall, reached out to shake Bob's hand.

"Hi Bob, I'm Tom Masters. You can just call me *Big Guy*. That's what the rest of this crew calls me." Again, everyone laughed easily.

Tom was a friendly fellow and Bob thought his height gave him a Rollie Fingers appearance. Rollie Fingers was a pitcher for the Oakland Athletics and was known for his signature handlebar mustache. Tom wore his thick, dark hair long like Rollie and he also wore a mustache. The only thing missing was the handlebar.

He was an easy-going guy with a quick sense of humor, which disarmed people to make them feel comfortable around him.

Lake Of Bays

This feels a lot like the Viking, Bob thought. *I like these guys. They can laugh at themselves.*

"Tom is head of our maintenance and land development." Van interrupted Bob's thoughts. "Both of you enjoy working with your hands. Tom also loves fishing, maybe as much as you, Bob. This perked up Bob when he heard that.

"Yeah, I noticed you brought your fishing gear," Tom said. "Maybe while you're here we can try to beat the record catch of lake trout on this lake."

"What's the record?" Bob asked.

"Fifty big ones," Tom responded. "Fifty lake trout?" Bob asked.

"Nope. Fifty pounds for one trout, caught right off Bigwin Island."

"Whoa, that's one huge lunker!" Tom was talking Bob's language. "You're on, Big Guy!"

The men laughed, not missing that Bob was already calling Tom *Big Guy.*

Tom could see he and Bob would get along just fine. "There's a lot of work to do around here so you and I are going to be spending mucho time together. Glad you came to Roothog, Bob."

Randy Wiseman spoke up next to welcome Bob to the island. "I'm the administrator of this ship, so, I get to do the paperwork."

"Oh, he does a lot more than that," Joe said. "Randy makes sure everything is running well, so we can play." Randy smiled.

"He's also a co-therapist in your program, Bob, but we'll go through all that tomorrow after breakfast. I'll meet with you first and then we will meet as a group to lay out your treatment plan."

Lake Of Bays

The last man to introduce himself was Simon Crabtree, the chief cook and the entire kitchen crew.

"It's nice to have you here, Bob," as Simon walked out of the kitchen. "You're welcome to join us. Eat up. My goal is not to have to deal with leftovers!"

The men returned to their supper and Bob joined them. He was so hungry he didn't care about his wet clothes. He had worked up a huge appetite in that storm and started to devour the food.

"I see you don't like my cooking," Simon said, smiling.

Bob had a mouthful of food so he didn't respond, but Simon heard his long, satisfied *Mmmmm*.

"Glad you like it, but I just feed the body. Van prepares the food that feeds the soul. He's the Bible teacher here on Roothog." Bob nodded. He knew the other men were not aware that he had prayed for Van about his decision to join the 2BeRealMen team as the Bible teacher.

"Breakfast is at eight," Simon announced. "Big day tomorrow so you all need to get some rest."

"I'll meet you in the office at nine," Joe added.

After the men finished up their meal with a slice of chocolate cake and a cup of coffee, Randy got up to show Bob to his room.

"See you guys in the morning," Bob said as he carried his gear upstairs and headed for the shower. It was dark early on Roothog and Bob was ready to fall into bed.

* * *

Lake Of Bays

As the hot shower warmed Bob's chilled skin, he thought about each of the men. He really liked how they seemed to respect each other and him as well.

His room was on the second floor of the lodge, at the end of the hall. It had a single bed, a wooden chair and a small table with a lamp. There was plenty of writing paper. There were three metal hooks on the wall for hanging his clothes.

The best thing about the room was the window facing the water. It opened onto the upper deck where he could relax and enjoy the view. The worst thing was the toilet being at the opposite end of the hall, just past Uncle Joe's room. Bob didn't mind a bit. In his mind he was in the penthouse suite!

Completely convinced Roothog was exactly the right place for him, Bob fell into a deep sleep.

11

The next morning Bob was up by the crack of dawn, eager to put on dry clothes and learn his schedule for treatment. Truthfully, he was more excited to see his surroundings in daylight because his primary reason was to scope fishing spots around the lodge.

Coming down the inside stairs, he noticed Simon in the kitchen and could smell a fresh pot of his smooth, dark coffee. It was Monday morning and Mondays would always start with scrambled eggs, bacon and pancakes with real Canadian maple syrup to top off the cakes.

"Hey Bob," Simon called out. "You're welcome to the coffee. You deserve it for getting up at the break of day! I'll see you in about an hour for breakfast."

"Thanks, Simon. You make great coffee."

"Made from clear, Canadian waters," Simon smiled. "Best in the world."

Bob walked outdoors into a new morning as the sun shined brightly. What he saw was remarkable. The Lake Of Bays is a clear, cold body of water with its deepest part at two hundred and thirty feet. He could see the shoreline dropping off to the deeper water just a few feet away from the lodge's deck. *Imagine the fishing off this deck, not to mention the lunkers I might find when I take the boat out!*

The lodge was well constructed and painted a soft muted green with dark brown trim. It looked peaceful. The second story porch of native cedar had an outdoor stairway in case Bob ever wanted to walk outside in the morning. *But that might mean missing Simon's great coffee,* he thought.

Circling around the lodge, he noted a second rowboat moored on land. Then he saw the pine trees on the island. One word came to Bob's mind. *Ugly.* He was pressed to see any hard conifers or other hardwood trees.

The forest of thick twisted trees pushed right up to the lodge on the lake's bank. The building was supported by strong pylons and a large rock ledge on the shore. Those trees, ugly as they were, did give a sense of privacy.

It was quiet, with the exception of birds singing. They were unbiased about the lack of beauty as the trees provided safety. Even though Roothog was definitely not a vacationer's dream, the lodge was an ideal place for the boot camp of 2BRealMen ministries.

Climbing the stairs to the porch, Bob found six wooden beach chairs. He sat down to catch the scenery. The porch railing consisted of cedar posts connected with a large gauge screen, presenting an unimpeded view of the water. The steps had traditional rails on them.

Perfect! Bob thought, looking out on the water.

He really liked the environment and was eager to explore the rest of the island wherever and whenever possible. Bob finished his coffee and began to hear rumblings from the men below. *Time for breakfast!*

At the table, Van led everyone in prayer to thank God for the food. This early in the morning, joking was at a minimum and of course there were no jokes about the food. How could there be? Simon's cooking was outstanding!

Lake Of Bays

As a chef, Simon's pursuit of excellence was persistent. His motto was *Pursue Excellence, Not Perfection.* He was also known to say, *whether in cooking or whatever I do, I'll do my best for the Lord.*

The men enjoyed their breakfast and everyone felt Simon's gift of encouragement in the way he prepared food with care and style. Bob, however, was puzzling over Simon's motto. He couldn't count the number of times he had heard or repeated, *"Practice makes perfect."* Could the pursuit of excellence be preferable to the pursuit of perfection? He planned to ask Simon about it when he got the chance.

* * *

After everyone finished eating, Bob followed Joe to his office on the lodge's first floor for his official intake meeting. It was located at the back of the building by the outside stairs.

Just inside the office door Bob noticed three signs hanging on the walls of the room. The first sign over the window read: **Surgery Without Anesthesia**. The next sign read: **No Secrets**. And, the last sign read: **None Of Us Is As Smart As All Of Us**.

Without a desk in the room, which seemed odd to Bob, the only furniture he saw consisted of a chalkboard and two comfortably padded chairs. As they walked in, Joe said, "Bob, pick any chair you'd like and have a seat."

For sure, Uncle Joe wasn't using Feng Shui to create a harmonious environment by simply placing furniture in the right position. Not with a sign that said *Surgery Without Anesthesia* in the room! Bob observed how one chair faced the window and the other chair faced the office door.

Lake Of Bays

What a predicament, right at the outset of the intake. *Where should I sit?* He wondered. *Facing the office door, I won't see the water or the shoreline. If I sit facing the window, I won't see anyone coming into the room but I'll have to look at a miserable sign that befuddles and bugs me at the same time!*

Bob hesitated. Instead of being like *Doc Holiday,* watching whoever walked into the saloon, he chose the chair where he could see the lake outside.

"Bob, I'm looking forward to working with you. Before we get started, I want to go over the 2BRealMen commitment to your treatment. It will provide a path to gauge how you are doing."

Confidently Bob replied, "That'll be fine, Joe."

"The first statement is to be faithful in working your own program for change by attending all individual and group sessions," Joe stated.

"I'm all in!" Bob said. Joe smiled at his fervor.

"The second statement is to enter your treatment and respect others by staying away from any explosive or violent outburst in or out of treatment.

"Hmmm. I'm in, but why is that statement necessary?"

"Do you see the sign above my head by the window?"

"Yes." Bob replied, curious.

"Have you ever had an outburst of explosive or violent anger in your life? I'm not looking for you to cite the incident, but only to say if you have.

"Yes, I have," Bob answered, shamefully.

"We may talk about that at another time, but for now this is what the sign means. To be straight out, nobody on the 2BRealMen team is going to wipe your hind end or diaper you. By the way you arrived last night I don't think you would want that anyway," Joe added.

JERRY PRICE & TOM ROY

Lake Of Bays

"You got that right, Joe." Just the picture of something like that happening to him was unsettling.

"Bob, my job is to disrupt any twisted thinking you have. I'm not here to destroy you, but I guarantee I will do my job. And when I do it, I'm not going to treat you like a child. You will be treated as a man and with respect.

At times it will hurt and there's no anesthesia to soften the blow. That's why the second statement in your commitment is your promise to stay away from explosive or violent outbursts. Whether you are actually in session or for some reason you go off Roothog Island, explosive or violent outbursts won't be accepted. If you are upset before you leave the island, you won't be allowed to go until we have a talk first. Are you committed to that, Bob?"

"You have my word. I will do whatever it takes to respect you and the men by keeping that commitment," Bob responded.

The third statement is to agree to participate in any psychological testing deemed necessary by the therapist and co-therapist in the 2BRealMen program. The purpose of the testing is to help clarify questions related to your issues in treatment."

"Absolutely! Whatever the doctor orders," Bob said, trying to sound compliant.

Immediately Joe went into accountability mode and said, "Bob, I want to address your choice of words."

Bob looked like the wind had been knocked out of him with that statement.

"I'm not a doctor," Joe stated, in a matter of fact way. I'm a primary therapist who facilitates your treatment. Before we meet again, write a report on what you were trying to accomplish by referring to me as a doctor who orders you. Are you open to doing that?"

Lake Of Bays

Bob agreed, but he became acutely aware of the sign above Joe's head. *I've been in this room for thirty minutes and this happens? Joe wants me to write a report about WHY I said it? This isn't going to be easy. I hate writing!"*

"Bob, the fourth statement is to agree to confidentiality within the program. If significant personal data is shared about others or if you go outside your accountability structure, it is grounds for immediate dismissal. Are you committed to this?"

"Yes, I agree. But am I hearing that right?

Am I hearing that applies to you or the other team members as well? Bob asked.

"Yes, you heard that right. There are no secrets within this group. None. We keep it here. Unless, and I emphasize *unless*, there's written permission to do so from the person the information is about."

"I'm IN!" Bob said with gusto. He learned he was protected by that agreement, as well as every group member was, and he liked it.

"Bob, the last statement in your treatment commitment is to agree to the discipline procedure regarding any failure to comply with your commitment. The client must come before the group to own up to their irresponsible behavior and seek the group's permission to return to the treatment program. If the client decides to quit, he will have to face the natural consequences related to any agreements with other organizations or with the courts.

Bob, before you answer this, we know you've asked to be a part of this boot camp. Van knowing you also helped in that decision. But some men we accept have been contracted by the courts, or they are here because of infidelity. When that happens their contract is mandated. Yours was not. I'm glad you asked to come. Nevertheless, it's a part of any man's commitment if they want to be here on Roothog."

"Yes, I agree to all of it, Joe. Thank you for telling me."

"Good. Here's the schedule with your treatment responsibilities. You'll be meeting with each team member during the week for a minimum of thirty-minutes. Then you'll have to write a report about your conversation and make copies for everyone. We must have it on that day, before everyone turns in at night. That gives us the leeway to address anything in the report we think needs to be dealt with in your next group or individual meeting with the men.

However, when you and I meet for your two-hour session each week, I will be the one who writes the report. Of course you will receive the report along with the men before we all retire for the evening. I will be looking for twisted thinking issues blocking you from moving forward as a man. I want you to be a STAR Thinker, which means Straight Thinkers Accept Responsibility. Here's a sheet of twisted thinking errors I'll be looking for within the reports or homework you complete."

Bob looked at the sheet and his eyes widened at the thought of what he was getting into. He saw ten twisted thinking patterns. The list read: Closed, Martyred, Inflated, Stubborn, Reckless, Impatient, Fearful, Manipulative, Arrogant and Possessive.

Every thinking error had two to five definitions to chart where a pattern of irresponsible decision-making was activated. Bob took a deep breath, somewhat overwhelmed.

"One more thing," Uncle Joe said. "I want you to memorize each twisted thinking error *word for word*. Start on the first two for the next time we meet on Thursday, and also for the team meeting this Friday morning at ten."

Lake Of Bays

The academics of it all created an internal storm for Bob. *Shoot! When it rains it pours,* he thought. *I'd rather row a boat in a windstorm than tackle this stuff.* Clearly, Bob's face reflected a sense of panic and trepidation.

Joe saw Bob's intensity level was rising and said, "By the way, you'll see we have also set aside breaks in your schedule for some quality fishing time."

Bob appreciated that part. After the meeting with Joe, he realized it was time to get down to business. Memorizing the twisted thinking errors felt like being back in school, and he was no fan of that.

Taking one more deep breath before leaving the intake session, Bob's dominant thought was it's back to the drawing table! I promised Al I wouldn't bail from my treatment and I won't. Struggling to mentally prepare himself for what was ahead, he stood to leave.

12

Bob left the meeting with Joe overwhelmed. He figured he'd be writing four reports a week for the first twelve weeks. That meant he was responsible for forty-eight reports. On top of that, he was required to go over Joe's reports and be ready to work with team members on issues that surfaced during those intensive sessions. When he added twelve to forty-eight and it totals sixty reports! Suddenly Bob had cold feet.

He remembered growing up in Coaltown, West Virginia, and being voted most likely to succeed in his Senior class of twenty five students. But nothing he had done in high school or since, including working in the coal mines and later in a steel mill, came close to this! The thought of all that writing terrified him!

Man! I can't believe all this thinking and writing! Plus I have to memorize the definitions of all those twisted thinking errors. Every stinking one, word for word! That doesn't even include the report I have to write for my next session with Joe about why I said what I did. All I said was I would do whatever the doctor ordered! It's only ten in the morning on the first day! If all that homework came out of a forty-five minute session with Joe, what's a two-hour session going to be like?

Bob felt like he'd been rung out and hung up to dry. He went up on the porch to settle down.

Lake Of Bays

*   *   *

What am I afraid of? Bob asked himself.

As he sat wondering, Simon's statement about pursuing excellence came to his mind. It helped him realize he had an issue with perfectionism.

I'm not sure what I write will be right or accepted, he admitted to himself. *I'm afraid if I put stuff down on paper, they'll all think I'm stupid. Trying to get into my own head isn't that easy! Asking why has never been my way of dealing with things. Having a six pack of Buds was how I used to deal with things. Right now I feel like I'm out on of one those ugly pine trees behind the lodge, hanging on a limb.*

Bob began wondering about other men who came through this program. He supposed the educated types weren't bothered by the reports. What he didn't realize was every client feared of putting his thoughts down on paper. Once those thoughts were on paper they were out in the open and the clients were forced to deal with their issues. Bob wasn't unique in this. People cover up their fears in different ways, but they all feel the discomfort when exposed.

Suddenly the sign in Joe's office came to his mind— *Surgery Without Anesthesia.* Was he trying to manage everything by attempting to be perfect? *I need to talk with Simon* he thought.

*   *   *

It was late morning and since the schedule indicated lunch was at noon, Bob figured he would find Simon in the kitchen. He headed downstairs and sure enough, he found him in the kitchen cutting up vegetables.

"What's up, Bob?"

Even though he had only been on the island a short while, in Bob's view Simon seemed to always be *up*. It made him feel accepted.

"Do you have a minute?" Bob asked.

"Sure, if you don't mind if I keep working. I've got a hungry crew to feed!" Simon smiled. "What's on your mind?"

"I've been thinking about your sign. What does that mean; pursuing excellence rather than perfection?"

"What triggered that question?" Simon could tell Bob was troubled.

"All my life I've been told that practice makes perfect." Bob began. "I don't understand the difference between excellence and perfection." He paused, hoping Simon would catch his drift and give him the answer he wanted.

"And?" Simon asked, refusing to bite on Bob's unconscious *pull* on him. He didn't miss the fact that Bob hadn't answered his question.

"What do you mean?" Bob asked.

"I get what you're saying about what you what you've been told all your life. But I asked what triggered that question for you. What's the real reason you're asking me that question?" Simon asked, while cutting up more carrots.

What the heck? Bob thought. *I just finished a session with Joe and now I'm in another one with Simon! I didn't expect this treatment would be everywhere I go on the island.*

Bob would soon find out this was true but he was going to have to experience it for himself.

Lake Of Bays

Recalling his session with Joe, Bob told Simon how he felt overwhelmed by all the writing he was required to do for the team. He admitted he was afraid of feeling stupid.

"Did you let Joe know how you felt before you left the session?" Simon asked.

"No, I didn't because it didn't really *hit* me until after the session was over."

"What are your choices for handling this besides coming to me with your question?" Simon asked.

"You want me to think about that now?"

Simon nodded his head as he poured roasted red peppers into the blender for the soup he was making.

Bob had a minute to think about his answer before Simon shut off the blender. Turning around, Simon smiled and lifted his left arm like a traffic cop, signaling to Bob he could talk.

"My choices are I could go back to Joe's office and let him know," Bob answered, "or wait until Friday's team meeting. Or I could write it in a report and copy it today for everyone to read."

"Okay. You decide, but get it done." Simon replied.

That was not what Bob expected. He had expected Simon to tell him which option was the best. Again, he felt like he'd been dropped off at a corner with no idea where to go. Alone. He would soon learn *feeling* and *thinking* are two separate issues.

Bob was trying to figure out why Simon wasn't helping him out when Simon spoke up.

"Here is what I believe is the difference between pursuing excellence verses perfection," he began. "I'm only going to give you three things today."

This is like the TV commercial that says, "When E. F. Hutton talks, people listen." Bob thought. He leaned in to hear the nuggets of wisdom Simon was about to speak.

Lake Of Bays

"First, perfection is being right and excellence is being willing to be wrong. Second, perfection is about control and excellence allows for being spontaneous. Third, perfection is pressure and excellence is natural."

"Now doesn't that sound like a chef's view? A good chef has to be natural, spontaneous and willing to be wrong. Without those ingredients, I could lose my mind cooking for you guys!" Simon laughed and Bob laughed with him.

"I can't talk anymore right now, Bob. I've got to get the main part of your meal ready. Those three comparisons might help you decide what it was that overwhelmed you after your meeting with Joe."

One more thing, Bob. The meetings you have with team members won't always seem official, but Joe means for you to write a report about conversations like we just had. I know we only talked about twenty minutes but that's how it rolls around here. The team will look forward to your report tonight." Simon turned back to his work.

* * *

After his conversation with Simon, Bob still felt overwhelmed. But one thing Simon said resonated. *Perfection is being right and excellence is being willing to be wrong.*

Bob decided to knock on Joe's door to tell him about his feelings and fears. Joe's office signs flashed back and forth in his mind, especially the one that said *No Secrets*. He was beginning to understand how everything needed to be on the table and out in the open for the right reasons. He wasn't aware of it yet, but that statement would eventually be life changing in his pursuit of excellence.

JERRY PRICE & TOM ROY

Lake Of Bays

  The office door was open and Joe was sitting on the chair facing the water. Bob knocked.
  "Come on in Bob! Joe said. What can I do for you?"

13

It was Monday evening. After stopping at Joe's office earlier to admit his struggle with fear, Bob went upstairs to write a report to the team about his conversation with Simon.

Even though he had been overwhelmed by his first full day, the team had taken it easy on him. But he sensed that would change. Or would it?

What's it going to be like further down the road if I'm already feeling like I've been here for weeks? It's only been one day! He began to get worried so before retiring, he decided to look over the schedule carefully to see what was ahead. According to the material he had been given, a typical treatment day included:

7:00 - 8:00 am Breakfast
8:00 - 9:00 am Meditation
9:00 - 10:00 am Journaling
10:00 - noon Free time
Noon - 1:00 pm Lunch
1:00 - 2:00 pm Exercise
2:00 - 3:00 pm Bible Study with Van
3:00 - 5:00 pm Outdoor Activities
5:00 - 6:00 pm Dinner
6:00 - 8:00 pm Free Time
8:00 - 10:00 pm Meditation, Reports
10:00 pm Lights Out

Lake Of Bays

Bob's personal schedule was slightly different. He would be meeting with Randy on Wednesdays from 9:00 to 10:00 am and with Joe on Thursdays from 9:00 to 11:00 am. The team meetings would be on Fridays from 9:00 to 10:00 am. His free time on weekdays totaled fifteen hours and in addition to that he had weekends off. That left thirty hours a week for other things built into his schedule.

Surprisingly, in Bob's mind the schedule didn't seem too bad. But that's when he noticed the exercise program.

What's this all about? Bob couldn't believe his eyes. *Wait a minute! What? They want me to row a boat around Roothog for fifty minutes every weekday! And right after lunch? What if I can't do that? What am I supposed to do when the lake ices over?* He wondered if he could trust this program. Remembering the storm he had encountered rowing to the island on Sunday, he was experiencing what mental health professionals called Gross Stress Reaction.

What he saw next took it up a notch. That's when Bob noticed the fine print under his outdoor activities. He couldn't believe his eyes! His eyes bulged at what he saw.

I'm supposed to be out there with Tom every weekday, cutting trees down, getting firewood and doing maintenance chores!

Apparently the men believed he was capable of doing more than he would have liked. Van knew Bob could handle hard work and bitter cold weather. Bob had worked for Captain Kurt on his commercial fishing boat on Lake Michigan. He believed Bob could do this as well.

Bob's reaction was not about his ability. It was about trying to avoid unpleasant tasks, one of his twisted thinking patterns he would learn about later. Just then he read something that calmed him down.

When the lake freezes, he read, I'm...what? His eyes lit up with joy. Ice fishing for two hours! Yes!

Before the lake was iced over, he figured he would be fishing off the dock during his morning free times. *If I have to do all that rowing right after lunch I'd better not take the boat out in the morning,* he reasoned. *I don't think I could drag my ass out there that much! But maybe I can get out after dinner and row to some hot spots to catch some lunkers!*

When the lights went out at ten, Bob fell fast asleep.

* * *

There were two choices on Simon's breakfast menu Tuesday morning. One was a Denver Omelet bake with ham, bell peppers, mushrooms, yellow onions and cheddar cheese seasoned with salt, freshly ground black pepper, garnished with avocado slices and chives. The other dish had a bit more fire. It was a three-egg Jalapeno, Bacon and Pepper Jack Omelet topped with sour cream and finished with cayenne pepper. Each dish came with a side of American fries, crispy around the edges, and a cup of Simon's smooth black coffee.

The men were livelier this morning. The conversation was buzzing and the jokes were flying. Bob felt comfortable, less like he was in a fishbowl.

Bob ordered his breakfast. "I'll take the Jalapeno Pepper Jack Omelet!"

"You'll be needing that extra fire, Bob! We're going to take a nature hike into those gnarly pines today. But don't worry, I'll be up wind!" Tom laughed.

"Then maybe you should order the Denver Omelet, Big Guy," Bob shot back, insinuating Tom might be the lesser man. The guys liked Bob's comeback, which they saw as a friendly jest.

"Just so you know, Bob," Randy piped in, "the Denver Omelet is a real man's meal, too, especially with a splash of tobacco sauce! Simon loads it up with so much ham he'll have Tom saying *'Oink.'*"

Bob didn't expect that coming from Randy, who was an 'administrator' type of counselor, which made it funnier to him. All the men laughed.

"Good one Randy!" Tom said.

Next on the schedule was an hour for meditation. It was a beautiful morning so Bob headed up on the porch. Van had given him a study in the book of Proverbs, and even though there was no pressure on Bob, he knew it would challenge Bob if he chose to do it.

* * *

The fear of the Lord is the beginning of knowledge but fools despise wisdom and discipline. That was in the first chapter of Proverbs. Bob was caught. He began to argue with himself, or maybe he was arguing with God.

If I get all the knowledge and wisdom I can, but jack with the discipline, does that mean I don't respect God? If that's true, I'm a fool according to this verse.

Bob thought about his reaction to the exercise program. What did they want by putting him in a tough position like that? What if he failed? And he questioned if he trusted the treatment.

The truth? He wasn't really thinking about his treatment. Bob was focused on his fishing and didn't want anything to get in the way of his agenda hauling in the big ones.

What if the rowing is all about discipline, he asked himself. He began to think more about this and how he didn't want to be known for being a fool.

The hour was up and it was time to journal. Bob wasn't quite sure what to journal so he chose to write about the breakfast time. One thing he noticed was how the men were able to be real during meals and not focused his treatment. However, he also knew something could come up and they would switch into accountability mode.

It will take me a while to get used to this, he wrote.

* * *

After lunch, Bob met with Van for Bible Study. They had been friends in Door County and they got along well. But here on the island Van was in the official position of the Bible teacher and Bob was interested to see how it would affect their relationship. They met at Bob's favorite spot, the porch.

Bob brought his bible and was ready to dig in but Van opened with a strange question.

"Bob. What came first, the chicken or the egg?"

"The egg," Bob responded confidently.

"OK, what about God's creation of man? If God created man first, and I believe he did, there was no egg. Right?" Van asked."Are we getting into sex education in our Bible study?" Bob asked, smiling.

Van laughed. "No Bob, even though the Bible has plenty to say about sex. The question is a dilemma about which event should be considered the cause and which should be considered the effect. Take a look at Ephesians, chapter four, verses seventeen through nineteen. Would you read that out loud?

"So I tell you this, and insist on it in the Lord, that you must no longer live as the Gentiles do, *in the futility of their thinking*. They are darkened in their understanding and separated from the life of God because of the ignorance that is in them due to the hardening of their hearts. Having lost all sensitivity, they have given themselves over to sensuality so as to indulge in every kind of impurity, and they are full of greed."

After he read the verses, Bob kidded Van, saying, "There's nothing in here about a chicken or an egg."

"Read verse seventeen again, would you?" Van asked, smiling.

After Bob read it, Van asked, "Here's where the chicken and the egg apply. If you are serious about change, what comes first? Is it *behavior* or *thinking*?"

A half smile slanted across Bob's face. "That's the end of our bible study for today. I'd like you to think more about this passage during your time on Roothog. But here's a tip for you."

Bob nodded in anticipation.

"You'll notice the Apostle Paul doesn't begin with changed behavior. He teaches the believers that change begins in their thinking. You see, Bob, our soul is redeemed but our minds are not. They need constant renewal."

Van had Bob's attention.

"A change in behavior doesn't necessarily mean you are changing. I'd like you to think about that."

"I will," Bob said quietly, nodding. He was beginning to understand that much more would be required of him in this program than he had initially thought.

Lake Of Bays

* * *

Tom Masters met Bob outside the lodge at 3:00 pm for his outdoor activity. He had read the small print on the schedule so he wasn't surprised to see Tom with two Christmas tree saws as well as a chain saw.

"I know you've read the schedule, Bob! Let's get to work," Tom said, cheerfully.

"The most difficult part will be negotiating the tree roots that cover this island. Be careful you don't trip and sprain an ankle. There is no other way to tackle what we are going to do. We're going to hike in about fifty yards from the lodge and the plan is to eventually clear an acre."

"An acre!" Bob's eyes grew large.

"Yes. One acre, man. We'll do as much as we can before the snow gets too deep. Without the wood we're going to cut, we don't have a way to heat the lodge.

"We do have solar power, but that's for the lights, the kitchen appliances and the water heater. Heating the lodge is on us. Today, we saw. Tomorrow we drag the wood back to the lodge to split with our new gas log splitter. You'll enjoy that."

"Are you ready?" Tom was already leading the way. "It gets dark early this time of year!"

It took ten minutes to carefully pick their way through the dense pine growth and over the tangle of exposed roots. They spent an hour trimming limbs off the trees before they could use the chain saw to cut logs from the trunks.

"Hey, Bob!" Tom called out. "Time flies when you're having fun, eh? Let's pack it in and head back. It's great to be alive when we know God is in control."

JERRY PRICE & TOM ROY

Lake Of Bays

* * *

During supper the men sensed Bob wasn't in the mood to talk. After another good dinner, all he had left in him was to sit on the dock and throw out a line. Exhausted, he was happy to just sit alone, hoping to catch something. He was tired but it felt good.

At eight he headed to his room to write his report and work on memorizing his first Twisted Thinking pattern. He had no trouble falling asleep at the ten pm lights out. It wasn't long before he was sawing logs, as well as in his dreams too.

14

Wednesday morning was Bob's session with Randy Wiseman. Every official counseling session, whether with Randy, Uncle Joe or the whole team, would be held in Joe's office. When Bob learned this in Monday's session with Joe, all he could think about was that empty room with two chairs and those signs above the door and the windows.

I wonder what a Native American Sweat Lodge is like, he thought, *because I sweat every time I go in that office.*

As enthusiastic as Bob was about being in the program on Roothog Island, he still had a difficult time with fear of the unknown and not feeling in control.

* * *

The session was scheduled at nine am. Bob showed up at ten minutes after nine. While waiting for Bob to appear, Randy had seated himself in the chair facing the Lake Of Bays and the familiar sign above the window which read *Surgery without Anesthesia.*

Bob greeted Randy but felt a tinge of irritation toward him for sitting in *his* chair. Of course no one on the team knew Bob had mentally laid claim to it, but he found himself forced to take a seat facing the sign which read *None Of Us Is As Smart As All Of Us.*

Lake Of Bays

Randy was all business. He handed Bob a paper called *A Scratch in The Table*. "I'd like you to read this list and tell me where you can identify yourself. Are you open to doing that?"

"Sure. Bring it on," Bob said, disingenuously.

Taking the sheet from Randy, Bob read eleven statements that identified a *twisted thinker*. He had never heard of such a thing and he had obviously never considered that he might be a twisted thinker himself.

The first statement was about how important EXCITEMENT is to a twisted thinker. It was not referring to normal excitement, like catching a big lunker in the Lake Of Bays. It was referring to being drawn to *forbidden* excitement, always ready and looking for a thrill. To a twisted thinker, life is about conquest and power.

Bob didn't acknowledge himself in the first description and kept on reading.

The second statement was how a twisted thinker ENDANGERS others by being aggressive and abusive.

The next descriptor explained how every twisted thinker does what's EASY, looking for short cuts and ways to pull the wool over the eyes of others.

He avoided looking at Randy, who was patiently waiting for Bob to see himself in at least one of the twisted thinking patterns. Bob was uncomfortable, thinking about that sweat lodge!

Bob didn't view Randy in the same way he viewed Uncle Joe or Tom Masters. Those men were big and they filled the room. Randy was a smaller guy, five foot nine and of slighter build. Bob sized him up, looking for any weakness he could exploit, secretly viewing Randy as an non-intimidating little Chihuahua. Randy, on the other hand, had already correctly sized

Lake Of Bays

Bob up as a man who liked to intimidate and be in control. Bob continued to read the list:

    EXPECTS TO BE SERVED
    EASY WAY
    EXAGGERATES
    ERRATIC
    EFFORT NOT THERE OVER TIME
    EMBITTERED
    EXPLOITS THINGS TO THE EDGE
    EVADES
    ENSLAVES OTHERS.

By the time Bob reached the end of the list, his perception of Randy was beginning to change. *That little dog is locking in on me like a pit bull,* he thought!

Bob was unsettled. But rather than admit to being threatened, he tried to act casual.

"I'm not sure any of this applies to me," he told Randy, a comment intended to change the subject. But the little Chihuahua wasn't biting.

"So are you saying you are about fifty-fifty on any of those descriptions? Am I understanding you right?"

With his chin pointed upward so he was looking down on Randy, Bob said, "I suppose you could say that."

"Good! Would you be open to discussing if it might be fifty one-forty nine?"

Bob was trying to read Randy for weakness, but found none. His poker face and matter of fact way kept the session on track.

Man! This guy isn't giving up on his list thing. Bob thought. "Sure. I guess so." Caught off balanced by Randy's

JERRY PRICE & TOM ROY

91

tenacity, he wondered if *this guy's bite might be worse than his bark.*

"You had an appointment at nine this morning, right?"

"Yeah.

"Did you notice when you came into the session, you didn't bother to give me an explanation for why you were ten minutes late?"

"Uh...Yeah."

"Do you know why you were late?"

By now this pit bull had Bob by the gonads.

"I don't know." *Maybe that comment will keep this conversation on a fifty-fifty level,* he thought, while smirking at Randy.

"It must be tough *not* to know."

Randy let that comment settle. They were looking intently at each other and Bob realized what he didn't know when he entered the session. Randy wasn't afraid of him and was ready to mix it up, man to man.

After a pause, Randy referred to the list again.

"Would you read out loud the last description of a twisted thinker's scratch in the table?"

Dropping his head, Bob read without enthusiasm, ENSLAVES OTHERS; *Need for power and control; I build myself up by managing others; my life is a series of events in which I build myself up; I have no long range goals, no lifetime ideas; I do not see whole picture, anything goes to expand my view.*

He looked up at Randy when he finished to see what his response would be.

"Bob, you were ten minutes late to your session. There was no traffic to keep you from being on time. There was nothing keeping you from letting me know you'd be late. You walked into the session like being late wasn't a big deal. I could also see that you didn't want me in the chair facing the water. Your irritation was written all over your face."

Boom! Mr. Bob Chadwick was just called out by the Chihuahua for activating Possessive Thinking, or a sense of entitlement known as an *ownership attitude*!

"What else you got to say, Randy?" Bob wasn't trying to hide his irritation this time.

"You just finished reading the last descriptor on the *Scratch In The Table,* Bob. The team is not on Roothog Island to waste your time. You are important and our job is to disrupt your thinking to move you toward a new way of understanding how to be a man.

The attitude you brought in here today stinks. Whether you realize it or not, you were trying to manage me by attempting to control this meeting. You think I don't know crap? It's only your third day and you arrive late for your first session with me? Where's the effort on your part? If you want to play power games, there isn't one of us on the team who is afraid to lock horns with you."

Bob didn't expect this kind of passion coming from Randy and he was impressed by it.

Randy pointed to a wall and asked, "Would you please read that sign out loud?"

"*No Secrets.*"

"Do you not see yourself in the statement that says you enslave others as a part of the way you think or make decisions? Were you aware that was what you were doing when you walked into this session? Whether you were aware of your thoughts or not, it's a pattern in your thinking, Bob. It's how you arrive at decisions when you enter the unknowns in your life. It is no secret. That's why you are here on Roothog. Your twisted thinking is getting in the way of you becoming the man you were built to be. Do you understand what this means for you?"

Bob gave a slight nod, his stomach in knots. "It means I'm at fifty-one percent."

Randy's eyes widened at Bob's halfhearted response and said, "The reality is this means you are much more than fifty-one percent. Joe and I have the job of convincing you of that, and it's the job of the team to keep you accountable. And, may I add, man to man!"

* * *

Before Bob left the session, Randy gave him a homework assignment.

"I'd like you to do something we call a *thought report*. You may put those thoughts into your report of this meeting if you like, killing two birds with one stone. The assignment is to reflect on what you were thinking before you came to this session. Write your thoughts about me, before and during our session. Tell the team about anything you fear. Are you open to doing this?"

"Yes."

"Our time is up, then."

15

Bob was reeling from his session with Randy. With only two hours before lunch, his priority was getting his *thought report* finished. An alarm was going off inside him as to how difficult this treatment was going to be.

He'd been in counseling back in Sandusky Bay with Lois but already he could see the way Randy Wiseman and Joe Hope worked with him was totally different.

Growing up in coal country, Bob had been taught manhood was determined by hard work, hard living and hard drinking. His self-assurance was based on how he could hold his alcohol. *And knowing how to bait a hook to fish,* he thought. Most of the men Bob had known lived by this standard, determining how Bob managed himself and others. But here on Roothog, the model for manhood was shifting.

2BRealMen started from the inside, where a man's word was as good as gold, where motives lined up with commitments, where authentic relationships were valued, where men respected others and had the courage to stand alone when necessary. Men were expected to take responsibility without being babied.

Most of all, the team's paradigm began with God. It was not about using God as a rabbit's foot for success but about moving into life's unknowns by trusting him. Starting from the inside was about going deeper, about exposing the direction of the thinking and the motivation behind the behavior of a man.

Lake Of Bays

It didn't take long for Bob to realize he would be held accountable to that standard. It would not be about his performance. *Maybe that's what Simon means by pursuing excellence rather than perfection*, he thought.

Troubled by what he saw in himself during his meeting with Randy, Bob decided to write the report without hiding or defending his ugly thoughts he'd worked hard to keep everyone, including himself, from seeing.

On Roothog, he would discover that having pride in his accomplishments were fine but they would not be the criteria for manhood. What mattered was whether he was accomplishing things for the right reasons, heading in the right direction and willing to risk genuinely loving people.

* * *

Bob went to his room to write the report, not wanting to miss what Simon prepared for lunch.

Standing in front of the mirror on the wall of his room, he stared, thinking, *No counselor ever shook me up like Randy just did. Imagine that, coming from that little Chihuahua.* By this time Bob realized he thought differently about Randy, even though his assignment was to write what he thought about him during the session.

My Thought Report
Date: November 5, 1975
Meeting with Randy

Assignment: Reflect on what I was thinking before I went to my session with Randy. Write what I was thinking about Randy during the session. Write about what I'm afraid of during and after the session.

Lake Of Bays

This will be short. Before I went to the session with Randy, I took my sweet loving time getting there. I've been tired from day one since arriving on Roothog. I was afraid I couldn't keep up, but the truth is I've been focused on fishing for lunkers and not my treatment. When I got to the session with Randy, I acted like meeting him wasn't a big deal and not important enough to respect. When I saw him in the chair I thought would be my chair during any session, I was pissed. But now I can see that was an assumption which became a secret because I didn't tell anyone.

Going into the session I saw Randy as a little Chihuahua and kind of a turd. But during the session, he showed being a smaller guy didn't mean he wasn't worthy of respect. I didn't expect him to be strong enough to deal with me, but he wasn't afraid of me or my crap. My fears are about wondering if I can make it through the boot camp.

When the report was finished, Bob ran copies off to give the men after lunch. *Learning about manhood is coming from places I never would have expected,* he thought.

*   *   *

Everyone was at lunch waiting for Simon's special chicken and wild rice soup, along with homemade garlic bread, lime Jell-O topped with mayonnaise and an ice-cold bottle of Coke a Cola to wash it all down. Bob was uncertain how his session with Randy would affect the atmosphere at lunch with the team, but in spite of his apprehension, the group's focus was on Simon's soup, which helped Bob feel normal in the mix of men.

Tom Masters whistled his approval. "Bring it on, Simon! My favorite soup of all time!"

Simon flashed Tom a huge smile.

"Come on, Bob." Tom urged. "Get ready for a feast. There's a tree outside crying for us to cut it down."

Lake Of Bays

"Gotta get my exercise in," Bob answered. "Today I'll be rowing to Fairview Island and back. You'll have to wait, Big Guy."

"You'd better chow down, then. You'll need an extra bowl of Simon's best!"

After two bowls of the wild rice soup, Bob made sure each man received his report in their office mailboxes before he got into the rowboat and took off toward Fairview.

The lake was calm. Instead of struggling with rough waters like he had the day he arrived at Roothog, the sound of the water splashing and dripping from the oars steadied his nerves. By the time he returned he was ready to meet Van at his favorite spot on the upstairs porch for a Bible study.

*　*　*

Van came up the outside stairs of the deck and greeted Bob. "Hey. Fella!"

"Van! Good to see you. I've been reading Proverbs."

"What chapter are you reading?"

"I'm still in chapter one trying to understand why Solomon wrote the book."

"What are you coming up with?"

"A couple things popped out at me. Verse two says, *to know wisdom and instruction; to discern the words of understanding* and verses five and six say, *That a wise man may hear, and increase in learning; And that a man of understanding may attain unto sound counsel: To understand a proverb, and a figure, the words of the wise...*"

"Bob, what words in those statements are mentioned more than once?"

"I see two. *Understanding* and *words*."

"Well then, let me ask you this. Within those three verses, how important are the use of words for understanding anything?

Bob spent time reading the verses again. He studied carefully and then blurted out, "They help in knowing wisdom and instruction. And apparently they improve a guy's hearing to increase his learning!"

"Yes! Bob. Let me teach you a study principle when you read the Bible that has to do with the use of *words*.

To understand a passage and the use of certain words in the Bible, there's a principle called *First Mention*. For instance, you identified two words that are mentioned twice in the passage you read. Let's try to understand what those *words* mean and how God may be using those words within a passage. Would you like to do this, Bob?"

"Absolutely!"

"Look at the first chapter in Genesis and count how many times you read *God said*."

Bob counted nine times where he saw *God said*.

"How many times does it say *God called?*"

Bob counted again and came up with four times. "How many times does it mention, "*God made?*"

"Five times," Bob said.

"Stay with me on this, Bob. It states *God said* nine times and then *God called* and *God made* for a total of nine times combined. That doesn't even include how many times it reads, *God created.*"

"What's your point, Van?"

"Nobody uses a word in a conversation, or calls out a word without those words coming from somewhere and going to someplace. Words are an expression of something seen or unseen."

Bob was curious now. But there was more coming from Van and he knew it.

"Let's look at John, chapter one, and find the phrase, *Word.*"

Bob had read the first three verses when Van stopped him.

> In the beginning was the Word, and the Word was with God, and the Word was God. He was with God in the beginning. Through him all things were made; without him nothing was made that has been made.

"Here's the principle, Bob. The *Word,* who was with God and who was God, is the outward expression of God. And there's that word *made* again, cited three times in those three verses. It means words are important because they show movement."

"Movement?" Bob asked.

"Yes. Movement! The expression of God in this case was with God and was God. In the beginning, he *made* everything in creation. Now that's movement, my friend. God is coming from somewhere to someplace!

So in the principle of First Mention, if you want to find out what a word means in the Bible, you can go to the spot in the Bible where it's first mentioned and get an idea of how important that word is.

In Proverbs chapter one, *words* denote that words come from somewhere and are going someplace. God who we cannot see demonstrates that principle by being the WORD who comes from somewhere – *heaven*, and goes to someplace – *earth*, as a person people can see. *Jesus!*

When we use words to speak, they're coming from the deeper parts of our hearts and minds, often from places we don't see or are not aware of. But when we use those words in conversations, they are going someplace and reveal why we're using those words. They become heard and seen.

Even the words we don't speak that swirl around in our thoughts are coming from somewhere and going someplace. Again. That's movement, Bob, just like we saw demonstrated in the first chapter of John about Jesus being the WORD in the flesh and in the first chapter of Genesis when the WORD *says*, or *calls* out, or *creates*. What was unseen is now revealed!

This is not a big secret, Bob. When we get this we're at the place where wisdom and understanding is available."

"So how does this apply to me being on Roothog?" Bob asked.

"Before I answer that, let's look at two more places in the Old Testament where we see *word* or *words* in the text. Would you read Deuteronomy, chapter eight, verse three?

> He humbled you, causing you to hunger and then feeding you with manna, which neither you nor your fathers had known, to teach you that man does not live by bread alone but on every *word* that comes out of the mouth of the LORD.

"Now look at Deuteronomy chapter eleven, verse eighteen. Read how it uses *words*."

> Fix these *words* of mine in your hearts and minds; tie them as symbols on your hands and bind them on your foreheads.

"Finally we can apply the principle of First Mention.

Although we didn't actually see *word* or *words* in Genesis chapter one, we know they are implied because we read, *He said, He called,* or *He made.* That can't happen without words.

Let me repeat the principle. A *Word* or the use of *words* always comes from somewhere and will go someplace. In these passages they are coming from a deeper place that is unseen and when used, they are expressing what's in God's heart. They expose who God is and what his character is like.

Likewise, the words we use in a conversation expose who we are and what is in our hearts. They show movement by revealing where we are coming from and where we are headed in relationships. They reveal things like pain, which can motivate us. Words are *that* powerful! *Words* are the major key to figuring out if we're open to sound counseling, understanding, wisdom and learning.

Here's where I'm going with this biblical teaching principle, Bob. I've read the thought report on your session with Randy. I'm not here to give you the type of counseling he and Joe will give you, but the Bible teaches that words are powerful and we are held accountable by the *words* we use. They are an expression of our hearts, or what I call the *deeper places in our soul*. Our inner thoughts are an unseen world, but those thoughts we embrace will eventually come out into the open through the words we use.

We may not always be aware of how our words impact others or where we are coming from when we use them, but we are responsible for thinking, saying and using them."

Bob was thinking about all this. Van waited for him to respond to the teaching.

"I get it, Van! You're saying I can know where I'm coming from and where I'm going through my use of words, whether I think or speak them. That gives me more than wisdom. It gives me an understanding I've never had or realized I could have in my decisions.

While I was rowing the boat to Fairview and back, I reflected on my report and I could see the twistedness in my use of words. It's not like some shadowy force I can't deal with. Right there in this principle of first mention, I can see if deeper change is happening inside of me.

I wish I had known this principle many years ago. But I promise you I will stick with this. I want to keep learning how to be a man who speaks from the heart without being angry and be able to love as well as you and Randy loved me today."

Bob's genuineness and openness to consider Van's *on the porch* teaching, moved Van. In fact, he was blown away by it.

Checking the time, Bob said, "I have to go help Tom take down some trees. Thanks, Van! See you later."

16

At exactly nine on Thursday morning Bob was at Joe's office for his first intensive. *There's no way I'm going to be late for this session,* Bob thought, recalling his meeting with Randy.

The night before, Bob finished the report on his meeting with Van and thanked him for the scripture teaching. He had never heard how the *words* a man uses, whether thought or spoken, could be the key to understanding where his thinking would ultimately take him in his actions.

What he didn't realize was how being with the team on Roothog would challenge the difference between him hearing a new thought and being able to flesh that out in his relationships.

As night fell, Bob spent time boning up on the first two twisted thinking patterns, while chewing over Joe's mandate to do the assignment *word* for *word*. He wanted to make sure he didn't come across as stupid.

* * *

"Come on in!" Uncle Joe called out when Bob knocked on the door.

Just like the first time, Bob saw Joe standing by the window.

"Where would you like to sit Bob?"

Once again, Bob chose the chair facing the window with the sign above it stating, *Surgery Without Anesthesia.*

"Bob, I'd like you to quote the first two twisted thinking patterns."

This guy doesn't mess around, Bob thought. *So much for small talk!*

"Uh, I am not receptive..." Bob began, when Joe interrupted him.

"I asked you to recite them word for word Bob. Would you start over please?"

Unnerved and intimidated, Bob hid his feelings and makes another attempt. Once more, Joe interrupted him.

Visibly shaken, Bob blurts out, "What do you want from me Joe?" he asked, palms up.

Eyeballing Bob, Joe calmly states, "I want you to quote these patterns word for word." Then, he sat back in his chair and waited on Bob to work it out for himself.

Bob settles down a bit and realized he had forgotten to introduce the name of the thinking pattern.

"Okay, I've got this," he said.

"**Closed Thinking**. 1. I'm not receptive 2. I'm not self-critical 3. I don't disclose information 4. I'm good at and pointing out and giving feedback on the faults of others 5. I lie by omission." Bob paused and began again.

"**Martyred Thinking**. 1. I view myself as a victim when I'm held accountable, 2. I blame social conditions, my family, the past, and others for what I do."

Bob's face had a slight grin.

"What's the grinning about Bob?"

Without shame and bobbing his head in personal agreement, he said, "I nailed it and I'm happy with myself."

"Didn't quite nail it Bob. I interrupted you twice. And like playing a game of horseshoes, you were close but there were no ringers. The third time you got it right."

Bob lost his grin, not liking what Joe said but he kept those feelings to himself. He had an image in his head of getting hit by a pitch and trotting to first base without looking at the pitcher or rubbing the bruise. There was no way that he'd admit to being hurt.

"Would you read the sign above the office door? Out loud, please."

Bob turned toward the sign. "No secrets."

"I'd like you to tell me what you were trying to accomplish the first time we talked by calling me *the doctor* and telling me you'd *do what the doctor ordered*?"

Even though he had done some reflecting on the assignment, Bob had trouble coming up with an answer. He began with his first thought.

"I think it was my way of saying I'm here to work."

"What else could you have called me?"

"I could have called you Joe."

"What can calling me doctor accomplish for you rather than calling me Joe?"

That seemed like a strange question to Bob. But he thought he had an answer that would satisfy Joe.

"I was letting you know you were the professional and I would do what you wanted me to do."

Joe goes deeper with Bob.

"Well then, if your treatment doesn't work for you, whose fault is it, since you were only doing what the professional wanted?"

Bob figured out what Joe was getting at and said, "Yours, because you ordered it."

"But if you call me Joe, then whose fault is it, if you fail in the program?

"Mine," Bob answered quickly.

"And if you called me Joe, why would that be different than calling me doctor?"

Joe wasn't letting this go. Bob felt like he was getting the third degree, and he couldn't come up with an answer.

"Are you open to hearing a few thoughts? Joe asked.

"Sure."

"Joe is who I am. Doctoring is what I do. When you decided to say you'd do what the doctor ordered, I felt like you were stiff arming me to keep me in my place. You came off like you were managing me, Bob.

But, if you called me Joe, you wouldn't have to anticipate being a victim because whether you realized it or not, I think you were setting yourself up to be one."

Bob's face was blank but inside he was thinking *he gets all that from me calling him doctor and saying whatever the doctor orders? You've got to be kidding me!*

"Are you open to tell me what you are thinking now Bob?"

Bob told Joe exactly what he was thinking. "I don't get how you come up with all that stuff."

"Do you want to go deeper into this?"

I can go deeper? There's more! Bob was stunned. But he wanted to know where Joe was going so he agreed.

"Yeah. I'd like to," he said, hesitantly.

"I read your report about your meetings with Randy and Van. I was pleased to see you beginning to respect Randy and thanked Van for his teaching. That shows me you were open to dealing with yourself.

Lake Of Bays

You've only been here a few days and I know you want to do well Bob. I know some of your history and the pain you've experienced. But, I've also seen in your reports that you're a man who doesn't like being questioned.

It's possible some of that is due to being shaped by a culture where children are to be seen and not heard. Maybe it comes from the distance between you and your abusive father. Maybe it's because you suffered being molested as a young man in the coal mine latrine."

Bob's eyes widened at that.

"Clearly you had to learn to survive. But along the way *you* made the choice to drink, to look at pornography and to live selfishly, particularly in your marriage. Before you arrived, Van filled us in on your history and it's obvious your life and your marriage were rocky. And it's undeniable you've been a victim in the past. But in trying to protect yourself from being hurt again, you became someone who hurts others. That's a twisted thinker, Bob."

Bob was listening attentively, absorbing all of it. Like Randy, Joe didn't beat around the bush. Their style was direct and sometimes painful. It was different than his friendship with Big Al or Van, but he also believed Randy and Joe cared.

Bob decided to take a chance at interrupting Joe.

"May I say something?"

"Yes," Joe answered, comfortably surprised by the interruption.

"I think I understand a problem I'm having with you. It's the same problem I had with Randy."

Joe was listening, highly interested in what Bob was going to say.

Lake Of Bays

"You're right about all the stuff you just told me. But I've never been around guys like you and Randy, or the other men on the team for that matter. I have friends like Van, or my friend Al, who are honest with me. But the friendship has been built over time. I also had friends in Ellison Bay who accepted me. I've never had anyone come at me like you and Randy, and in such a short time.

Joe could see the wheels turning in Bob's head and waited for him continue. He believed Bob thought no one with authority would listen to him or care about him. It was time to hear what Bob had to say.

"I'm not looking to excuse myself but I came here looking for some of the qualities in you men that I experienced with the guys in Ellison Bay and with my friend Al. I may be wrong about this, but I didn't have a chance to warm up with Randy or you.

Looking at that sign above your head scared the shit out of me and I was on guard with you two. You guys weren't kidding about not applying anesthesia to this process. It's intimidating and I don't like feeling that."

Joe smiled at Bob but not because his remarks unsettled him. Clearly Bob has made a decision and Joe was waiting for what he hoped to hear.

"You're right, Joe. I don't like being asked to explain myself. My fear is that you or Randy couldn't handle me asking you questions."

"Where do you think that came from Bob?"

"I don't think I've ever opened up to anyone other than three men—Van, my friend Al and my son, Joey." Speaking Joey's name broke the dam in Bob.

Joe waited as Bob wept for his son.

"May I see if I understand what you're saying?" Joe asked.

Bob nodded.

"You're having trouble believing Randy and I care about you because of our approach. We don't have the time to build a relationship with you like you had with Al or Van, or with your son. We have the tools to dig deep. We call it *care-fronting*. I'd venture to say no one in authority has ever done that for you. You're here on Roothog because you're at a crossroad and you're facing an unknown future. You have to make a decision.

Bob pauses, takes a breath and says, "I'm here to learn about being a man from all of you. I'll not keep secrets about what I'm thinking or feeling. I'm jumping in with both feet!"

"Great decision Bob! I can only imagine how hard it's been for you to get to this. Before you leave today's session, may I ask you to do two more things?"

"Yes," Bob agreed, adding, "*Uncle* Joe."

Joe sensed *respect* in Bob's humor and laughter fills the room.

* * *

Joe handed Bob an evaluation that would measure the patterns he would use to think successfully and the twisted thinking patterns he would use to be irresponsible in his decisions.

The evaluation took Bob about twenty minutes to complete and then Joe said, "I'll reveal the results tomorrow, when the team meets for the first time."

Bob nodded and asked, "What else would you like me to do before I leave today?"

"I'd like for you to read the sign that's over the door, out loud."

"*None of us is as smart as all of us.*"

Lake Of Bays

"I'm committed to that statement, Bob. All of us are accountable to each other on Roothog. Thank you for opening up in your thinking today and embracing your healing process. It's one day at a time.

17

After a long first week on Roothog, Bob was able to accomplish more than he thought he could. He was into the flow of the island and kept up with Tom Masters, cutting firewood from those gnarly pines for the coming winter. And, although he goofed up while reciting the first two twisted thinking patterns in his intensive with Joe, he surprised himself by memorizing what he did.

There had been a few uncomfortable encounters in his counseling with Randy and Joe, but they had been balanced by Van's Bible teaching. By focusing on his use of *words*, Bob was still dazzled at what they revealed about where he was coming from and where he was going, both in this thinking and his actions. He knew it would take time to pull it all together.

Simon was an important part of the team as well, though he used food more than words. His food spoke volumes about love and respect. There was no doubt Bob was eating well. Next to Lois, Simon's cooking was the best he'd ever had. It made Bob realize how Lois had tried to communicate her love through her cooking. *I was too busy being a pompous ass to see it,* he thought.

Bob was also getting into the rhythm of his daily rowing. Occasionally, he'd drop a line in the lake to reel in a fish. But this was Friday, and he would be facing every 2BRealMen Team member in his first group meeting.

* * *

JERRY PRICE & TOM ROY

Lake Of Bays

Bob's first team meeting commenced at nine sharp on Friday morning. The minute he walked into the room he knew it would be different. There were six folding chairs forming a circle in the middle of the room. In addition there was a new sign near the office door, which read *I am a Twisted Thinker. I use twisted thinking to hurt others. I will not hurt others or myself again.*

Joe Hope began the session by asking Bob to stand and read the new sign *out loud.* Bob hesitated and then stood up slowly. He tentatively read the sign, without emotion.

"Bob, this sign is your twisted thinking *watchword.* Read it again, please. And this time would you put some heart into it?" Joe asked.

The team sat while Bob stood and read the slogan a second time.

"That was better, but I'd like for you to read it one more time. This time, imagine shouting through a megaphone on the upper deck, announcing it to the whole Lake Of Bays!"

Bob cringed at the thought that anyone on the lake might hear him. The team saw him shoot daggers at Joe with a look, but waited patiently for him to do what Joe asked.

After reading the sign a third time with what he considered extra effort, Bob sat down, giving Joe a look that clearly said, *There! Are you Satisfied?*

Tom asked, "What the heck is the scowl all about Bob?"

"I didn't like the idea of reading this *that* loud." "Did anything else bother you about the exerciseBob?" Randy asked.

"I've never admitted being a Twisted Thinker and now I'm vowing I won't hurt others or myself again?

It doesn't make sense to me."

Simon asked, "What were you feeling when you read it?"

"Like I wanted to craw into a hole and hide. Ashamed. Scared."

"Of what?" Van asked.

"Me! That the whole world knows I'm a twisted thinker. I've read all those definitions and they fit me lock, stock and barrel. I know I've hurt people. Reading that sign makes me feel like like a liar. How can I promise I'll never hurt others again?

"So what if you say you don't *want* to hurt others again?" Randy asked. "Or how about you *hope* you don't hurt others again? Or you won't *mean* to hurt others again? What's missing in all those words, Bob?"

Again, the team waited patiently for Bob answer. When he looked up, he saw Simon smiling at him.

"What are you smiling at Simon?"

"You, Bob. I'm smiling at you. I believe you've got this and I'm enjoying watching you struggle for the word you want."

"*Commitment*! Bob looked at Randy. The word is *commitment*! None of what you suggested Randy requires commitment on my part. They dance around it but all of those statements give me an out."

"Bingo!" Simon shouted.

Everyone was smiling at Simon's excitement that Bob had figured it out. It was like his enthusiasm in the kitchen when he found just the right spice to give his food that extra kick.

"You nailed it, Bob," he said. "I knew you had this. Commitment *is* the word!"

"Are you open to saying that watchword like it's your commitment?" Joe asked. "I didn't ask you to quote that sign just to please the team. We are asking if you are willing to commit to not hurting others. It doesn't mean you are promising you will never hurt anyone again. It means you are committed to rejecting any twisted thinking that hurts others."

"Yes, I am," Bob answered, smiling because he sensed what was coming next.

"Great! Now read it again, with *commitment*," Joe said. "But this time I'm going to ask the team to stand with you."

It was a high moment for Bob to know he wasn't promising to never hurt himself or others again. Instead, he was giving his commitment to identify twisted thinking and *not go there. Period.*

Suddenly, Bob connected Van's teaching on the importance of *words* with what Joe and Randy were searching for from him. Recognizing the direction he headed in his use of words was a huge concept to grasp.

He would eventually come to accept how his *Whys* were more important than only behaving right. It's about believing and seeing what's in his heart—the good, bad and ugly of it. Choosing to be alive, embracing relationships with responsibility and love. More than that, it was about allowing himself to *be* loved by God and others like the men on the 2BRealMen team.

"Okay men. Lets take a *pit stop* and come back in ten minutes," Joe said. "Simon! Could you put some fresh coffee on for us?"

"Can do, Joe."

* * *

The team gathered again in Joe's office, sipping steaming mugs of coffee. "Men, yesterday during Bob's session, I had him take the Star Energizer Evaluation test." Turning to Bob, he asked, "Would you be willing to read the results to the team?"

"I would!"

Lake Of Bays

Joe passed the evaluation results to Bob. "The first page is your successful page. It shows the responsible thinking patterns you'll favor in decision-making. Would you read your top five successful thinking patterns in sequence?"

"*Reliable, Honest, Open, Relaxed and Steady,*" Bob read.

Joe begins to teach Bob as to where this is all going.

"Your top three patterns are your "go-to" patterns for successful thinking. In fact, when you worked through Randy's questions and came up with the word *commitment*, it was clear to me that you were concerned about being reliable, honest and open in your thinking with us.

Now, would you read your relational achievement skills, which are connected to each of your top five successful patterns?"

"They are being *Loyal, Trustworthy, Reflective, Accountable* and *Purposeful*."

"Each skill supports the sequential thinking pattern it is connected to. For example, when you are *reliable* in your thinking, you value being a *loyal* person. When you are *honest* in your thinking, you value being *trustworthy* and when you are *open* in your thinking, you value being *reflective* or taking time to work through things. When you are *accountable* in your thinking you are more *relaxed* and when you are a *steady thinker* you are *purposeful* in what you do.

Here's another thing. You will find yourself looking for the same patterns and skills in others. When you don't see them, it can cause relational conflicts, which puts you at the threshold of Twisted Thinking."

Bob was listening carefully and the team could see he was taking it all in.

"Would you be open to some feedback from the team?" Joe asked

"Sure am. This stuff is fascinating to me."

Randy spoke first. "Well Bob, after lunch we're all going to take some time off. But your time will involve only one thing and that's taking the rowboat out and catching fish! Why is that you ask?"

"Because it's Friday and Friday night is fish and chips!" Simon answered. Turning to Bob, he said, "We don't eat unless you catch some *lunkers,* as you call them. We're counting on you to use all those successful thinking patterns and activating your relational skills!"

Bob and the team burst out in laughter.

"The pressure is on!" as Bob returns the banter.

When the conversation resumed, Tom mentioned he thought the Star Energizer was right on in describing Bob's thinking when he's being responsible. "I see that when we're working together taking down pine trees."

Van thought the evaluation was dead on with what he knew about Bob during his time Ellison Bay. He saw this kind of thinking going on in Bob's work ethic and said he was open to taking coaching from him when they met back at the Viking Grill.

"Now, would you read the results on your unsuccessful page," Joe asked. "This will reveal your twisted thinking and the ways you hurt others to protect yourself."

"Yes."

Bob wasn't looking forward to this part. He was aware it would be painful. His inner sin styles were about to be exposed and there would be no anesthesia.

"*Reckless, Manipulative, Closed, Fearful, and Stubborn.*" *Sick!* Bob thought.

"The rule of thumb is the same," Joe said. "Those patterns are the polar opposite of each responsible thinking pattern on your successful page. They are your dark side. If you cross over the threshold to these thinking patterns, you'll come across as lacking empathy and without remorse for any irresponsible decision you make."

In that moment every wicked and foul thing he had done to his wife flashed through Bob's mind, like the time he had tripped and spilled hot coffee on his infant son, leaving permanent scars. He had blamed Lois. The unsuccessful page described him so accurately it was overwhelming. But Joe gave him no reprieve before the next question.

"Tell me, Bob what are the success blockers connecting you to these twisted thinking patterns?"

Bob's stomach was knotted so tight he felt like he had just taken a punch from Mohammed Ali.

"When I'm thinking *recklessly*, I'm *disloyal*. When I'm a *manipulative*, I favor being *deceitful*. When I'm *closed* in thinking, I'm *superficial* with people. When I'm thinking *fearfully*, I will find a way to be *unaccountable*, and when I'm *stubborn* in my thinking, I'll be *unyielding*."

Joe explained what it meant to activate a twisted thinking error.

"When you find yourself in a twisted thinking error, even if is it only for a few seconds, you'll have to make a choice to activate that thinking, or replace it with a polar opposite responsible thinking pattern.

If you activate the error, making it the path to your decision-making, that thinking pattern will eventually come out in your behavior for all to see. If you shut it down, people will see that in your behavior also.

Here's the kicker, Bob. It's possible to have good behavior being generated by twisted thinking, too. Looking only at behavior, as the criteria of change can be misleading to anyone looking for deeper changes in the direction of your thinking.

That's why you need to be in relationships where questions can be asked to see if your thinking is changing. That's called accountability. And accountability calls for consequences if you fail to line up your thinking and behavior to be responsible.

It may only take seconds to make the decision to activate thinking errors or reject them, but the consequences of those decisions can last for years. It's that critical, Bob."

Randy asked, "Would you be open to hearing how that happened in today's session?"

"Yes," Bob answered, somewhat open.

"Do you remember when Tom asked you what your scowl was about and you told us you didn't like reading the slogan that loud?"

"Yes."

"But you didn't tell us what you were thinking in that moment. Right?"

"That's true."

"Do you recall what you were thinking? I have an idea but I'd like to hear from you."

"Yeah, I remember. I thought about sending Joe a message through my glare. I was thinking, "There! Are you satisfied now?"

"Bob, What was your payoff for not actually saying those words to Joe?" Simon asked.

"I felt strong giving him an attitude to lighten up. I didn't want to get into words with Joe."

Van asked, "What message did you send to the team when you gave him that look? Van asked.

Bob didn't expect that question from Van. He saw how his disrespect toward Joe also showed his disrespect toward Van and the group.

"It was disrespectful to everyone."

"That's true Bob, but I'm asking where you were going with that look and not what you were being."

"I'm not sure Van."

"Would you be open to the team telling you where we think you were going with the look?" Tom asked.

"Yes." Bob was curious.

Tom started the *go-around*.

"I think you were showing you could control Joe with looks. I also think you were *manipulating* us with your tough guy crap to try to send us a message to back off. You do that when you're uncomfortable. It felt like a threat."

"I think you made Joe the perpetrator and yourself the victim." Randy added. "Maybe you were thinking if you could treat Joe like an umpire you think just screwed up a call, you could get a team member on your side. I would have had more respect for you if you had just said what you were thinking. That way there wouldn't be any secrets about what you were trying to accomplish."

Simon added his thoughts next. "I didn't see you move toward excellence in that decision, Bob. Why? You took the easy way out of something that was disagreeable to you. There was no *effort* in giving Joe a look. Work for you would be to tell Joe what you were thinking. Frankly Bob, you came across as a stubborn little brat to me."

Bob looks at Van because it's his turn in the go-around.

"I think you are afraid of Joe and avoid any accountability to open up your thoughts to him. You don't like being in a place where you think someone has control over you, and especially someone older than you, like Joe."

Bob was caught. He looked over at Joe, but this time the look on his face was more receptive than before.

"Well, Bob, it looks like you got the full enchilada! The guys are all holding you responsible for your game playing. Did it surprise you that simply sending me a look exposed every one of the twisted thinking patterns you favor?

"Yes," Bob answered, embarrassed.

"Your decision to send me a look sent all of us a message that you didn't want to put any work into your relationships with the team. When you aren't being superficial, I enjoy you, but that look you gave me was faked and unmanly."

No one in the room needed to say any more. No one rescued Bob and he didn't want them to. He thanked them for speaking honestly with him.

"I appreciate each of you for telling me what you saw. I'm sorry I disrespected you. I see how I tried to take the easy way out. And yes, I see how wimpy I can be."

* * *

There was one more thing on Joe's mind. "Bob, before we go would you be willing to do an exercise with the team?"

Bob waited to hear what it was. Would you be willing to lie down on the floor and allow the team to pick you up and raise you over our heads?"

What? Bob thought. *That's a shift from exposing my dark side to these guys!* He decided not to ask why, however, and just lie down on his back. Each man found a pressure point on his body: one on the neck, two on each side and two men at his feet.

Lake Of Bays

Bob remained stiff bodied, with his arms folded, as the team bent over to pick him up. After feeling a little nervous, to his amazement, up he went!

The team held him there for several seconds and an unexpected calm came over Bob. Even the Chihuahua showed strength, not faltering in his support. This was known as the *Roothog Trust Boost*.

After the team lowered Bob, Joe asked him if he'd be open to reading the sign above the door.

"None of us is as smart as all of us!"

The meeting was over. Bob's homework was to write what he was thinking and feeling during the boost.

As uncomfortable as it was for Bob to be *care-fronted* by the team, he knew he had been respected by their forthrightness. Strangely, there was an excitement about being with these men he hadn't experienced before. It felt like family and the men seemed like brothers.

For now, Bob's focus changed to catching lunkers for the Friday night fish fry. He looked forward to hanging out with his *brothers*.

18

MY ROOTHOG TRUST BOOST by Bob Chadwick

When the guys had me do the Roothog Trust Boost, I was concerned about being dropped. A small man I'm not, and being lifted high above their heads put me in a position where I couldn't see anything except the ceiling. But I decided to do it anyway, feeling curious and afraid at the same time.

With my arms folded across my chest, up in the air I went! I didn't expect to feel comfortable but I did. In spite of my issues with Randy and Joe during our sessions, (or should I say, in spite of my issues with me), I trusted them to do the right thing.

I learned the guys cared about me. They were being themselves with me and they wanted me to be real with them. I'm learning this isn't about performing to get God's love and favor, or theirs. Its about being a part of a team while learning how to be a man without losing my individually. All of this hit me at the top of the boost in a matter of seconds!

After they respectfully set me back down on the floor, I actually believed I wasn't just some guy they were working on. We were working

Lake Of Bays

together and I felt like part of the team. I had never experienced that before.

* * *

It had been three weeks since Bob's *Trust Boost*. From that moment forward, he was consistently productive and focused on being more receptive with the men. He wasn't afraid of being self-critical to make sure he didn't hurt them. Maybe it was saying the twisted thinker's watchword that helped, but however he got there, it was clear Bob had turned a corner in his treatment.

Another thing became apparent on the 2BRealMen team. Bob worked at not keeping secrets whether they were intentional or unintentional. He considered hidden agendas as poison to his system and started to relax with being himself.

Van's studies in Proverbs continued to help Bob gain perspective on being a sound and balanced thinker. What really caught his eyes was when he read what God hates in Proverbs 6:16-19.

> These six things doth the LORD hate: yea, seven are an abomination unto him: A proud look, a lying tongue, and hands that shed innocent blood, An heart that deviseth wicked imaginations, feet that be swift in running to mischief, A false witness that speaketh lies, and he that soweth discord among brethren. KJV

Memorizing his twisted thinking errors reinforced what the proverb said and helped Bob recognize when the *twist* was happening—even *before* it could happen in his decision-making.

Writing reports and turning in the homework kept him accountable and reliably accurate.

Lake Of Bays

Catching fish went beyond casual recreation. A few times, Bob had taken Tom out on the lake, with the goal of breaking the Lake Of Bays record for landing a fifty-pound Trout.

While they were fishing together, Bob discovered Tom's dream of working as a college baseball coach or having a ministry in the Fellowship of Christian Athletes. He also dreamt about influencing men in professional baseball too.

"Who knows Bob? God may open some of those doors for me one day, but for now, I'm right where He wants me to be. In this boat, with you and looking to reel in the biggest lunker ever on the Lake Of Bays!"

"Man Tom. I like the way you dream about baseball, ministry and fishing. But Mr. Recreation Director, I'm the one who's going to catch that lunker!"

Floating off the shores of Bigwin Island, where all the rich and famous holidayed, they began to laugh hilariously at Bob's challenge.

Then Bob started bantering in a tone of camaraderie. "But I consider myself a privileged man just to be working with you Tom; chopping down those ugly pines for fire wood."

"Ha. It's in the mundane where we see God at work Bob."

"What did you say?"

"I said, it's in the mundane where we see God at work. Why'd you ask?"

"My buddy Big Al, said that to me before I left Sandusky. He told me to look for that on Roothog. Hearing you say it reminds me of another thing he used to say. *God is present in the ordinary.*"

"Keep that going for ya Bob. Because baby, tomorrow we chop!"

Both of them had another good laugh but the profoundness of what Al and Tom said was life changing for Bob's attitude development.

Twisted thinkers don't like to give effort in doing anything they find boring, disagreeable or mundane. They think living in a responsible way is unexciting and unsatisfying. But Bob felt clean inside himself and was happy to be held accountable by guys who cared about how he thought and behaved, man to man.

He was beginning to understand what Big Al had been saying all along. Maybe he was right. It was possible to experience God in the least likely places, even on Roothog Island.

* * *

A month had passed since Bob arrived on the island. The fall weather would be ending but before the snow arrived, Joe Hope gave Bob a long weekend off from the island. He decided to use the extra time to visit Sergeant Ben Smith in Denbigh, about two and one half hours East of the Lake Of Bays.

I can't shake this feeling of wanting to see Sergeant Ben. God, would you give me this time to have a talk with him?

The sudden death of his son, Joey, plus the painful task of identifying his body, had left Bob completely overcome with shock. It had been two years since then and he wanted to tell the Sergeant how much he appreciated his kindness in the way he dealt with him.

It was a crisp morning and the sky was bright. It didn't take long to get off Roothog and on the road, once Bob knew he had a mission. Stopping briefly for gas and some beef jerky, he was soon heading east on highway 28 toward Denbigh. Bob had no idea how important this trip was going to be for him.

Lake Of Bays

* * *

Bob parked in front of the Denbigh Royal Canadian Police Station and slowly walked toward the entrance. Everything looked the same as before. It was late Saturday morning and fortunately, the station was open.

As he went through the front door, standing right before him, and bigger than life, was Sergeant Ben Smith! No one else was in the building and he sensed this was a moment only God could have arranged.

"Bob Chadwick!" The sergeant reached out to shake Bob's hand, recognizing him instantly. "How are you doing?"

Before Bob could answer, he said, "I'm so glad to see you! I'm not usually here on Saturdays. This is amazing you showed up here right now."

Bob couldn't get a word in.

"Please sit down," the sergeant continued. "I have some incredible news to tell you! For several months after you left I tried to call you but there was no response."

"I'm sorry Sergeant, I was…"

"Doesn't matter Mr. Chadwick. You are here now. We have the results from your son's autopsy."

"What! I thought you said the autopsy didn't reveal anything. There was no sign of injury, no explanation how a healthy, athletic eighteen-year-old could have drowned."

"That was true Mr. Chadwick but a few weeks later I read an article on a condition many young adults had, who were dying in the USA and Canada. It was originally connected to older folks, but new research discovered it was happening with them too. On a hunch, I decided to do another analysis on Joey's body."

"What did you find?"

"Your son had a condition called ASD or Atrial Septal Defect. The phenomena had been discovered in 1968. His drowning had all the markers of what was known as a *hole in the heart*."

"A hole in the heart?"

"Yes, the way I understand it, the heart has two sides, separated by an inner wall called the septum. A hole in the septum between the heart's two upper chambers is called an atrial septal defect. It's a congenital heart defect that occurs when normal heart development is disrupted during the first eight weeks of pregnancy."

"Are you saying Joey had this problem at his birth?"

"That's right. An atrial septal defect allows blood to pass from the left side of the heart to the right side. The, oxygen-rich blood mixes with oxygen-poor blood, and some oxygen-rich blood is pumped to the lungs instead of the body. Most atrial septal defects occur by chance with no clear cause."

"Could you put all of this in simpler terms?"

"Yes sir. Basically it means if the hole is large and permits a lot of extra blood flow to the right side of the heart, the heart and lungs will become overworked. It may cause symptoms like difficulty breathing, shortness of breath and tiring easily, especially when active.

Mr. Chadwick, when Joey was born, ASD was unknown in the medical world. Had they known, it would have been caught and repaired with surgery. While growing up, the right situation never came about to discover your son's condition.

Lake Of Bays

When Joey went swimming that night with the girl he met on the shore, he had fallen into a cold lake and lost his ability to breathe. I believe that's when his heart gave out Mr. Chadwick. That's why there were no marks on his body indicating injury or foul play.

Bob Chadwick began to weep, both with sorrow and relief. On the one hand he missed Joey and longed to see him. On the other hand, this information released Lois and him from any parental failure. Oh, he knew he had failed his son in many ways. But the cause of his death wasn't about their failures.

Curiously, the only thing going through Bob's head was *wondering if Lois and Joey met in heaven to talk this out.*

He questioned if she had peace knowing as hard as she worked to care for Joey, that in the end, God gave them eighteen terrific years with their son. That there was nothing either of them could do to stop what had happen. That Joey went out of this world and into the next, happy. And how one day, they would all be together again, as a family unit.

"Thank you Sergeant. This helps a great deal with what you've told me. I also want to thank you for your kindness. Even though I had a hard time when Joey died, I always felt respected by you and it's an honor to know you."

The sergeant nodded appreciatively.

A lot has happened since that night Sergeant, but I wanted you to know I'm over at the Lake Of Bays on Roothog Island. I'm working with a group of men who are helping me become the man I'm built to be. Joey's life and death is a big part of why I'm there. Your story has confirmed that I'm at the right place at the right time."

Lake Of Bays

Bob and Sergeant Smith left each other with a huge man hug, but there was one more stop he had to make.
Lake Weslemkoon!

19

Lake Weslemkoon was just forty minutes from Denbigh in the direction of the Lake of Bays. Bob felt compelled to return to the cabin where he and Joey had stayed. It was a trip he had planned to celebrate his son's high school graduation and his signing a contract to play professional baseball with the Chicago White Sox organization.

The thought of returning to the cabin no longer held Bob hostage. The horror of Joey's death followed by the painful task of identifying his body had paralyzed Bob's soul. He had left Lake Weslemkoon without hope.

Bob's life fell apart after that and he never wanted to relive the memories of that dark time. But with what he had learned from Sergeant Smith, Bob sensed a new connection to Joey. He now saw Lake Weslemkoon as a sacred place, similar to the Sandusky Cemetery where he had his talk with Lois. It was the last place he and his son had spent time together and he had a strong desire to see it again.

On the way to the cabin, Bob grieved the loss of his family. But he also felt hope. *Nothing is going to keep me from enjoying my son,* he thought fiercely. *Not even the cabin or the lake where he died. He's alive and in heaven! I'll see Joey and Lois again.*

The fear of returning to the place where his son had died had lost its power over Bob. He couldn't wait to get to the cabin to have a talk with his son.

* * *

Lake Of Bays

There was really no way Bob expected the same cabin he and Joey had stayed in to be available. He was thrilled to learn it was open and quickly reserved it for two nights. After carrying his few things inside, he found himself on the pier. He stood there a long time, recalling two years earlier where in a broken rage after Joey's death, he had heaved his son's duffle bag into the lake. This time there would be no need for Southern Comfort to numb his pain.

It was close five o'clock in the afternoon and already growing dark. The fall colors were bright against the setting sun and there was a chill in the air.

Joey, for a long time I wore the guilt of not being able to protect and save you from drowning. Then I was mad at you for doing something stupid and irresponsible. Whatever I could do to get control never worked. You were gone and I couldn't bring you back. I searched for what you believed about heaven and life after death. It wasn't until I gave my self to Jesus that I realized how much I loved you son. Lord, thank you for the eighteen years you gave me with Joey. I'm looking forward to seeing you and hanging out with Lois and our son again.

The tears Bob shed after letting Joey know he was okay were mixed with the joy of anticipating eternity, and the understanding that God was leading him into a new life. But, it was still hard to think that Joey died of an Atrial Septal Defect. Nothing was left of his family other than the memory of his wife and son along with his hope for eternity.

Everything about the cabin brought back memories. Bob recalled the special way he and his son had bonded at the cabin. In his mind he could smell the fresh fish cooking and hear the conversations they had. Then, he had an uncommon sense of being able to see his son soon. He had no idea where that came from and quickly let it go.

It was getting late so Bob decided to head into town. The smell of rotisserie chicken greeted him as he walked through the door of Wannamaker's Grocery Store. He knew it wouldn't compare to Simon's cooking but he added one of the chickens to his cart along with fresh bakery buns and a few other items. As he headed to the cash register he saw something that stopped him dead in his tracks.

* * *

A small boy, about fifteen months old and full of energy, ran down the aisle right in front of Bob. He stared, speechless. The boy was the image of Joey at that age!

The boy's young mother was behind him, pushing her cart, when she looked up and saw Bob staring at her son. What happened next was a miracle!

"Mr. Chadwick?" The young woman's eyes were wide with surprise.

"Who are you?" Bob was trying to figure out how this young woman knew his name. What she said next would change his life.

Smiling, she answered, "My name is Lucinda. I can see Joey in you, Mr. Chadwick. And I can see our son in you, too.

"Our son?" Bob was dumbfounded." What do you mean?"

Bob's head was spinning. Was he really in a conversation with the young mother of a boy she claims is Joey's son? Could this boy be his grandson? How could this be? His mind was full of questions. Everything was happening fast but to Bob it seemed to be moving in slow motion. Bob didn't know how he could feel so confused and so excited at the same time.

He pulled himself together and spoke to Lucinda. There was a bench outside Wannamaker's and Bob nodded his head toward it.

"Do you have time to sit outside and get acquainted?"

"Yes, I do."

Bob was struck by a joy he couldn't explain as they sat down to have a conversation.

"What's this little guy's name, Lucinda?"

"Joey Junior," she replied.

Just then Joey started babbling in words no one but he could understand. Bob was smitten and laughed at the way children are so innocent and real. He nodded his head up and down as if he understood, choked with tears of exhilaration. Bob was full of awe. *What timing! I have a family!*

Little Joey took to Bob as if he'd known him all his life. Nothing about Bob intimidated or threatened him. He climbed up on Bob's lap, looking at his mother for approval.

"How did all this happen, Lucinda?"

She began telling the story of meeting Joey on the night he died.

"Joey was rowing his boat past my dock in the early evening. We waved and it didn't take long to get to know him. He got out of the boat and we sat on the dock and talked for hours. He was such an open and friendly man. We talked about his contract with the Chicago White Sox. He told me the fishing trip to Lake Weslemkoon was to celebrate his signing the contract. He thought the world of you, Mr. Chadwick. He loved you very much."

Bob hugged Joey close, full of emotion.

Lake Of Bays

"I know it sounds crazy but I fell in love with him that night. Joey told me he wanted to be with me the rest of his life. One thing led to another and we ended up making love.

We were so happy but it was getting late. Joey said he needed to go but would come back the next day to introduce me to you. He pulled out a picture of you two from his billfold and gave it to me. That's how I recognized you. Joey hugged me one more time and then..." Lucinda started to cry.

"What happened next?" Bob asked quietly. He knew it would be as hard for him to hear as for her to say.

"It was really dark. When Joey got up he tripped on the dock and fell into the water. I heard splashing and waited for him to climb up on the dock but suddenly it got quiet. I didn't know what was happening and I felt so powerless!" Her eyes filled with tears.

"I ran to get help but by the time the police got there it was too late. They questioned me about what happened and as soon as it was daylight they began a search for his body. Later I was asked to go to the Denbigh station to identify Joey's body.

Not long after that I discovered I was pregnant. I wondered about you but wasn't able to contact you for some reason. I wanted you to know you had a grandson. I prayed God would allow us to meet one day.

My family lives here at Lake Weslemkoon and they enjoy being around little Joey. I'm certain they would like to meet his grandpa," she smiled.

"Thank you for telling me all this. I can only imagine how powerless you felt that night, but I learned something today about what caused Joey's death that might help." Bob noticed Joey Jr. was getting tired.

JERRY PRICE & TOM ROY

Lake Of Bays

"I'll be in town for another day. Would you and Joey be available to come out to the cabin tomorrow? We could talk more then.

"Sure," she nodded, grateful. "How about around noon, before Joey's nap time?"

"That would be great!" Bob gave her directions to the cabin before they said goodbye. He gave Joey a squeeze and then spontaneously asked Lucinda if he could give her a hug, too. *Wow! That really made me feel like a grandpa,* he thought, after they left.

* * *

That night Bob slept more peacefully than he could remember. So much had changed in such a short time and he was overwhelmed by God's goodness. Suddenly his life felt like it was in living color!

He had struggled so much in the last two years, but not all of it was because of Joey's death. Much of his pain was his own doing. He began to understand that God was working in his life on two levels.

On one level he had experienced the consequences of his own sin and arrogance. On a second level he knew God was always working behind the scenes, almost like being undercover, to express his redemptive love for him. Meeting Lucinda and little Joey at the grocery store—*out of nowhere*—was proof of that to him.

One level didn't negate the other in God's pursuit of Bob, and he understood more clearly how God was always working, even in the mundane.

The next day Lucinda and Joey Jr arrived at the cabin a few minutes before noon. He had fixed a modest lunch and as they sat down at the table she told him how grateful she was that God had brought them together. He could not have agreed more.

Over lunch Bob was able to explain to her the condition Joey had with his heart. He tried to keep it simple by referring to his condition as a *hole in the heart*. He explained how it put stress on the heart and caused extreme fatigue. She seemed very interested.

"So that's what happened to him that night?"

"Yes. No one knew about this condition at the time, Lucinda. But if you're concerned about Joey, Jr, there is a way to check it now and it can be corrected with surgery."

Lucinda was quiet. "God knew, didn't he?"

"I believe he did. I don't understand the why behind Joey's death, but I do believe God is in control."

She nodded.

"One thing God has done is to give me a new family. You have my commitment that I'll stay in contact with you, Lucinda. I want to be a part of this little guy's life. He has some Lunkers to catch in the future."

"Lunkers?" She asked.

"I'll tell you all about that another time," he smiled.

They visited for over three hours and it was as if they had always known each other. Bob told her about his time on Roothog Island and the accountability program with men who cared about changing his thinking and his behaviors.

She was impressed. "I like that at any age people can change for the better. Thank you for your example, Mr. Chadwick. It gives me hope," she said. Then she added, "I think Joey was a lot like you."

Bob was touched by Lucinda's comment.

Hesitating a moment, she said, "Um, what should we call you? Bob or Papa?"

"Yes!" Bob smiled. "Whatever you are comfortable with, Lucinda."

* * *

Bob explained to her he didn't have much time off from the program on Roothog Island, but he would do everything he could to stay connected.

"I'm there for at least another two months," he told Lucinda. "Winter weather might make it hard to travel. Plus my job is to provide firewood for heat and fish for food, so that will keep me pretty busy. But I'm looking forward to coming back and meeting your parents."

That pleased Lucinda.

Before Bob could say goodbye, she hugged him and said, "I love you papa. See you next time."

He hugged her back and picked up little Joey, whispering something in his ear. His mother couldn't quite tell what he had said but she caught something about him becoming a real man. Joey babbled something in return and Bob was sure he heard *Papa*. He smiled and hugged the little guy, trying to memorize everything about him.

Bob couldn't wait to tell the guys on Roothog what God had done for him! For the first time ever, he felt whole.

20

On Monday morning Bob was ready to head back to Roothog Island. Before leaving, he decided to write a report about his weekend away. He wanted to bring the team up to date, but he knew if he didn't sort it out he would fly into the lodge so pumped up he wouldn't make sense. This way, Bob had time to process everything that had happened. Besides, checkout wasn't until eleven.

Report by Bob Chadwick

I'm grateful for the weekend break from Roothog. It became an event way beyond my imagination. My mission was to stay at the cabin where I last saw Joey, before he died two years ago. I wasn't sure what would happen but, in my heart, I wanted to connect with him.

First, I met Sergeant Smith at the Denbigh Police Station and thanked him for his support in the darkest hour of my life. Then the Sergeant handed me a new autopsy report describing what caused Joey's death. He had a condition called ASD or a hole in the heart, a birth defect that was unknown in the 50's when he was born.

Then I reserved the cabin on Lake Weslemkoon where Joey and I stayed to fish and celebrate his contract with the Chicago White Sox. Just being back there helped me overcome a giant in my life.

What happened next was way beyond my wildest dream. I was getting some food at the Wannamaker Grocery Store. I

Lake Of Bays

don't know how to say this any other way except to say God had a plan to dazzle me! He arranged for me to meet my grandson! I had no idea I had a grandson! His name is Joey Jr. and his mother's name is Lucinda Martin.

It's an unbelievable story! I'm eager to tell you the rest when I get back to Roothog.

God had literally changed Bob's life in one weekend and Bob was humbled. He was already committed to the program on Roothog and didn't mind the hard work. Even though he had met Lucinda and Joey Jr., he was still on board with it. In fact, now that he knew he had a family, he was even more committed to becoming the real man he was created to be.

Bob was full of joy and peace on the return drive to the Lake Of Bays. Yes, there was still sadness about losing his son, but he had a new reason for hope. In fact, he had a purpose for living like he'd never known before.

Big Al used to talk about how God can move through different dimensions so we can know him in deeper ways. He also talked about looking for God in the mundane, but this weekend I have no question that God moved to a different dimension with me! I can't really explain it, but he did.

Bob's view of God had been damaged from his days at *His Word Community Baptist Church* in Coaltown, West Virginia. Later, when Reverend Rico, the pastor in Sandusky, Ohio, betrayed everyone's trust, it really derailed Bob. Looking back, Bob could see God had been with him, putting Big Al in his life to guide him through it.

God, you've never left me alone. You've taken me from Coaltown to Canada, and given me a daughter in law and a grandson. Who would have thought I'd be at this place in my life right now? Thank you!

JERRY PRICE & TOM ROY

140

Lake Of Bays

* * *

Bob rowed the boat to the Roothog dock and was eager to meet everyone at the supper hour and feast on another one of Simon's excellent meals. He was eager to place a copy of his report in each man's mailbox before the meal so they could read it. Otherwise he would have to wait until the next morning to talk about it.

Delicious aromas greeted him as he walked into the lodge. Simon came out of the kitchen and welcomed him back.

"Hey, Bob, you made it back. Great to see you!"

"You too, Simon! What's on tap for tonight?" "Salisbury steak with gravy and *Poutine*, or Canadian French fries, and cheese curds. Coca-Cola, of course, to wash it down. Good comfort food!"

"Sounds like good grub!" Bob said, in his best West Virginia twang. "See you in about an hour."

"I hear you, Mr. West Virginian!" Simon fired back, laughing.

The men were in good spirits as they gathered in the dining area.

"Hey Bob," Tom shouted across the room. "Rowing across the lake won't be so easy in a few weeks. It's gonna be tough to row through ice."

There was easy laughter in the room.

"No problem big guy," Bob shot back. I'll just get a sled!"

"Good! You can use it to haul all that wood you're gonna have to cut up. There's a lot of work to do, buddy. It's gotta last all winter!"

Lake Of Bays

It felt good to be back. Bob realized he had missed the guys. He was eager to share his news with them but even without it, the lodge felt like home. *These guys are family.*

After the meal, Joe stood up.

"Before you leave, Bob, I'd like to give you a chance to tell us about your weekend. All of us received your report and I know this is a change in your schedule, but we'd like to hear more from you now, if you're open to it."

"Yes, I am."

"First of all," Bob began, "I want you all to know how much I appreciate each of you." He had to stop for a minute because of unexpected tears.

Even though he had only been in the program a short time, it seemed like he'd always been there. He knew he was just starting to live this new life and he knew he had a long way to go. But he treasured the relationships he was building with these men and considered them brothers. He had learned he could be himself and they liked him anyway. In fact, they had treated him with genuine love and it was time to open up his heart.

Looking each man in the eye, Bob told them what he thought of them. He wasn't thinking about what he should or shouldn't say. He had no agenda and wasn't trying to impress anyone. He just poured it out.

The team listened and Randy looked up with a genuine smile and said, "Thank You."

Simon got up from the table and went over to give Bob a hug and slap on the back. Van couldn't contain himself. Nodding his head up and down, he gave Bob a thumb's up and a "Praise God!" Tom gave him a bone crunching man hug, followed by Randy, Van and Joe.

Lake Of Bays

"Thank you for letting us see the real you," Joe said. "We love you and we *like* the real you, Bob. It takes a strong man with a tender heart to do what you did."

Bob was humbled, but in that moment he experienced *the joy of the Lord*, a phrase Van used often.

Afterwards, Joe said, "Now, let's hear all about your weekend!"

* * *

The next few weeks flew by and Bob was able to make another trip to Lake Weslemkoon to see Lucinda and Joey Jr. at the end of the month.

Tom was right. It was getting colder and ice was beginning to form on the lake so he was allowed to use the motorboat to get off the island. After all his rowing, it felt like a graduation for him. This trip was important for Bob because he was going to meet Lucinda's parents.

The drive gave Bob time to review what he had learned. He had stayed committed to the 2BRealMen team treatment. He had faithfully memorized every twisted thinking pattern, learning to thread through them to understand where he was coming from and where he was going in his mind. It helped him identify if his thinking went dark.

Bob often quoted the twisted thinker's watchword, an exercise to build up empathy levels. He was feeling comfortable in his own skin and staying real. He knew he was a forgiven man. There's something about hope that warms the bones, he thought, even on a cold Canadian winter day.

* * *

Lake Of Bays

Bob enjoyed meeting Lucinda's family. John and Jean Martin were warm and welcoming, and they clearly loved little Joey.

When Joey saw Bob, he ran toward him with his arms up, babbling. Lifting him into his arms, he looked at Lucinda.

"Did he just say, *'Up, Papa'?*"

"I think so!" Lucinda nodded, laughing.

He hugged his grandson and put him down so he could go back to playing.

Bob and John hit it off well, especially when talking baseball. As it turned out, John was a Montreal Expo fan and liked ribbing Bob about the Expos finishing fourth in the National League East that year, compared to the Giants' fifth place finish in the National League West, respectively. Bob enjoyed John's crisp, Canadian accent and his easy sense of humor. It was comical to be discussing the better team when neither of the teams finished high in their divisions.

Unfortunately, it was a short visit. A storm was moving in and Bob decided to return ahead of schedule.

"I'm not sure when I will be finished with the program," he told Lucinda, "but if they release me before Christmas I'd like to visit again." He hugged each of them goodbye, whispering *I love you* in little Joey's ear. The snow was coming down by the time Bob reached the Lake of Bays. He made it back to Roothog Island before the worst of the storm.

* * *

Bob knew he was in treatment but he also saw himself as a student. He enjoyed having regular discussions on Van's Bible teaching with all of the men.

Lake Of Bays

Randy and Uncle Joe kept the sessions on task. It was as if they were on a search and seizure mission for any word, thought, or attitude that didn't pass the test for living responsibly and loving others.

Bob was glad to be learning about himself with men who were safe to be around. It didn't matter anymore what chair he sat in during his counseling. He understood Joe and Randy were watching for *ownership or entitlement* attitudes. He learned those attitudes were the embodiment of evil and they immediately took him to the dark side of twisted thinking.

When twisted thinkers have attitudes of ownership or entitlement, they perceive people as objects that belong to them. They have no concept of the ownership rights of others. For them, sex is not about intimacy but it's used for power and control.

Bob knew that particular pattern of twisted thinking had deeply damaged his relationship with Lois. And it was strange how identifying a chair as *his* could reveal the same darkness of heart and soul. But it did and activating an ownership attitude was something he watched for on a regular basis in his new foundation for manhood.

* * *

On a cold Friday in the middle of December, Bob sat down with a steaming mug of coffee in Joe's office. He had spent most of the day cutting down trees and splitting firewood, and he had been able to get in a couple of hours of ice fishing not far from the lodge. He was waiting for the team session to begin when Joe got the meeting started.

"Bob, we have something on the agenda today we would like to discuss with you. It has to do with where we believe your treatment has taken you."

He didn't know what they had in mind but he was listening carefully.

They talked about Bob's growth as a man. He was learning to examine his decisions, major or minor, to determine if anyone would be hurt. That included his language and his humor.

They could see he was becoming comfortable with himself. He wasn't trying to impress anyone or present himself as anyone other than himself. They enjoyed his honesty and openness.

Bob was blown away by the sincerity of the men. These were words from brothers and friends!

Randy mentioned he noticed Bob was more willing to embrace uncertainty, especially after God amazed him with the discovery of his grandson. He was more open to whatever God wanted for him.

He also said, "I like that you didn't try to impress or manage us with *God talk*. But I did enjoy talking about God with you."

"I agree with Randy," Van said. "You didn't play that card and I think that's why I grew to respect you even more than in the days back in Ellison Bay."

What these men were saying meant a great deal to Bob and the fact they were seeing change reinforced his resolve to keep moving forward.

"So here's what we're thinking, Bob." Joe got straight to the point. His direct approach was refreshing and the men exchanged smiles.

"Tom is leaving us in the spring. He's been given an opportunity to coach college baseball in Indiana. Tom, would you like to tell Bob what the team has discussed, since you will be leaving us?"

Elbowing Tom, he added, "No pressure, *Big Guy*!"

The men laughed.

"We would like you to consider taking over my work here on Roothog. You would become a team member with 2BRealMen and develop your own maintenance and recreation program. Your job would be finding creative ways to help other men who participate in the program. I believe you would add your own unique style!"

The men laughed again and nodded in agreement. The love in the room was tangible and Bob had never experienced anything like it. God was taking him into yet another dimension, right into his longing. He wasn't about to waste time thinking about it.

"Yes!" he shouted. "Yes!"

"I had a feeling that's what you would say!" Simon jumped up and headed for the kitchen, returning with a double chocolate layer cake. "He is the only man who calls my food grub and gets away with it."

Again, there was laughter in the room.

"There's no one I'd rather see join this team than you, my friend. This calls for a celebration!"

Everyone enjoyed Simon's cake but the friendships in the room were even better. Joe made sure Bob knew he had the weekend off and that his treatment would be officially completed the week before Christmas.

After the holidays he would be meeting with the team to discuss the agenda for the next few months. After that, he would be serving Jesus on Roothog Island!

Lake Of Bays

* * *

"Hello. Lucinda? This is Papa. I have fantastic news!"

And we know that God causes everything to work together for the good of those who love God and are called according to his purpose for them.

Romans 8:28

BOOKS BY JERRY PRICE & TOM ROY

The Chadwick Bay Series

SANDUSKY BAY
A Novel

Sandusky Bay follows a generational journey of three men: a grandfather working the coal mines in West Virginia, his steel mill working son in Ohio, and a grandson growing up with the baggage of previous generations. Join the journey of these three men as they find themselves trying to navigate the worlds of work, women, family, and life's unexpected trials. "Sandusky Bay thoughtfully and creatively exposes the misconceptions of what many men have learned real manhood looks like. Through the characters in this story, you see both the good and bad potential of the decisions you make and how they can affect the ones who are following you through this journey on earth.

> Chris Singleton, ESPN Analyst

ELLISON BAY
A Novel

The journey continues...the second book of a 2BRealMen trilogy involving the Chadwick Family. After a hard start in Coaltown, West Virginia, a rocky marriage and the tragic death of his son, Bob Chadwick now finds himself desperate for direction and the motivation to move forward in life. *ELLISON BAY* continues to follow Bob in his journey toward responsible manhood personifying the mystery of life, under insurmountable odds, and generational family failures. Join us as we continue to work through his issues of life, faith, women, and family to discover his purpose for living.

JERRY PRICE & TOM ROY

Lake Of Bays